Original Sins

Aja Holland

Willow River Press is an imprint of Between the Lines Publishing. The Willow River Press name and logo are trademarks of Between the Lines Publishing.

Between the Lines Publishing
9 North River Road, Ste 248
Auburn ME 04210
btwnthelines.com

First Published: December 2021

ISBN: (Paperback) 978-1-950502-63-9
ISBN: (Ebook) 978-1-950502-64-6

Library of Congress Control Number: 2021950336

Original Sins

Aja Holland

Chapter One

"I'm fairly certain this hardly measures up to the culinary choices you had back in New York," Dr. Jonathan Manx said, then turned from Reggie to his colleague, "nor even what you had available to you in Philadelphia."

Dr. Francis Cole nodded good naturedly. "I do miss a good cheese steak, if that's what you mean by 'culinary choices'."

Manx laughed. He had a rich, full laugh. "Hardly haute cuisine, true, but where better to get a Philly cheese steak than Philly, yes?"

Again, the good-natured nod from Cole.

It was hard to disagree. The Clipper may have been the best to offer from among Diamond Cove's few eateries, and there was a clear attempt to give it an upscale look: paneled walls, latticework partitions between the booths, tabletop candles, a Woodstock era survivor with a gray ponytail and what seemed to be the same jeans he'd worn in his Vietnam protest days strumming an acoustic guitar over in the bar section, but the food was no better nor worse than some of the upscale diners Reggie had known back in Manhattan.

Manx and Cole were a study, Reggie appraised, not so much in opposites as complementary parts. Manx was older, middle-aged, but obviously accomplished at being a well-maintained middle-age: trim inside his three-piece suit, a full head of gray-streaked hair brushed back in a proud lion's mane, his tanned face graced with a professorial salt-and-pepper Van Dyke. Even with the touches of gray, there was an energy to Manx that radiated a youthful vitality.

Cole was a good fifteen years younger, giving him just a few years on Reggie. He was slimmer than Manx, but it was a subtly athletic litheness, and it seemed to go with his quieter, low-key demeanor. Not shyness, exactly -- Reggie's own professional experience told her no one could be any kind of mental health professional and be shy -- but a reserve, as if he was carefully picking when to speak and what to say. Manx liked the presentation of authority and solidity in his three-piece suits and immaculately coiffed mane. Cole was more relaxed, unobtrusive with a blazer over a black T-shirt and jeans, his loose and long dark red hair falling attractively across his forehead. Manx liked to fill a space; Cole filled the small, precise gaps Manx left.

But each in their own way, Dr. Regina McLaren considered, was more than pleasant company, and even more pleasurable as they vied for her attention.

Oh, it wasn't that either of them had anything serious in mind; they barely knew her. It was more instinctive; two men, one woman, they were going to compete. Men were men and this was how men were; they couldn't help themselves, she thought and fought off an amused smile. Even with some of her patients back in New York, she'd observed the same dynamic, and had, early on in her practice, learned not to wear skirts in her sessions, to always let a male patient walk in front of her knowing that otherwise his eyes would be locked on her five-days-a-week-in-the-gym taut rear.

Still, she had to admit, mildly reprimanding herself (although without much conviction), she didn't really mind two attractive, intelligent men mildly battling for her attention.

"Now that you've been officially hired," Manx said, reaching down under the table, "I think the occasion deserves a toast." He came up with a paper bag, reached in and slipped out a bottle of wine. "The cellar here leaves a bit to be desired," he said, signaling to the waitress for a corkscrew, "although to be accurate, it's not really a cellar. It's just that small rack behind the bar. Thank you, dear," he said to the waitress, taking the corkscrew and began twirling the bit into the bottle's cork. "A friend I have out on the West Coast sends me a bottle now and then, the kind of things a bit hard to find in this part of Maine. Well, actually, anywhere outside of Portland, eh, Francis?"

"For myself," Cole said, "I don't mind the simplicity." He looked to Reggie to see which way she was leaning... the simple life or Manx's urbanity.

"This is supposed to be a very interesting pinot noir from the Russian River valley. If it lives up to my friend's description, I think you'll enjoy it. Certainly, the occasion deserves something special. Even you would concede that, eh, Francis?"

Cole smiled at Regina. "It *is* a special occasion."

The cork popped free, Manx gave it a quick sniff, then poured himself a taster's dose, took a sip, obviously showboating his expertise. "Oh, yes! Definitely on point for the event!" He poured out glasses for each of them, then raised his own. "To the now completed faculty -- the entire faculty, such as it is -- of the Psychology Department -- such as it is -- of the University at Diamond Cove." They clinked glasses, took a sip. Manx looked expectantly toward Reggie, smiled with a certain gloating satisfaction when she nodded approvingly, then turned another look toward Cole; got one up on you, junior.

Again, Reggie smiled inwardly… men!

"Once we settle on your class schedule and office hours, we have to work out your clinic hours. As I explained to you in your interview, we each put in volunteer hours at the local public health clinic as well as with the university's counselors. This part of the state is fairly rural, low-income, and since the mills closed, not many options for the locals. That's a rather toxic brew; isolation plus rural poverty and frustration equals dysfunctional families, sometimes deeply broken families. Sadly, a lot of the people we find ourselves dealing with at the clinic as well as the school are our own students. Most of them are small town kids away from home for the first time."

"I thought *this* was a small town!" Reggie said, surprised.

"For some of these kids, this is Metropolis!" Manx chuckled.

"Portland's only --".

"About an hour or so south, yes, I know," Manx nodded, still amused, "but an hour north of Portland or even less heading west and you're in what could tactlessly be referred to as 'the boonies'."

"It's a different scale," Cole said with a sad, agreeing nod. "Your neck of the woods, you take a two-hour bus ride and you're playing the slots in Atlantic City. A two-hour ride from here and you're either in timber country or potato fields." Cole shook his head. "No surprise, then, depression runs through this campus like the flu."

"Ironically, this works to our benefit as we try to establish the department," Manx went on. "Our psych majors will sit in on some of our clinical work as observers, get to see firsthand the kind of work they're presumably interested in. Which brings to mind a question."

Reggie nodded for him to go ahead.

"I never asked during the interview, it wasn't particularly relevant, my focus was more on your qualifications. You were in private practice back in New York. Big city psychologist, you must've been doing quite well."

"Why is this relevant now?" Cole asked. "She's already hired."

"Curiosity, Francis. It's the nature of what we do… curiosity. Aren't you curious?"

"We all left somewhere, Jon. Even you."

"True. I was always primarily an academic, but only ever as faculty. I couldn't say no to the chance to build, from the ground up, a psychology department, even a small one at a small school. That's *my* story. Regina, I don't want you to feel obligated to share yours, but --"

She was already shaking her head that it was fine, but she did so with her eyes locked on her wine glass, her long, slender fingers twirling it nervously by the stem. She didn't know if Manx had noticed, but she glanced up and found Cole watching her slowly rotating glass, then he looked up, caught her eye, gave her a small, barely noticeable smile, part comfort, part understanding; it was ok for her to refuse.

"Do you remember the Manhattan Study?" she asked Manx.

"Back in the 1950s, wasn't it?"

"Cornell, 1950-1960," Cole said.

Reggie smiled, impressed.

Cole smiled back. "The estimation was that between the people currently receiving some sort of help, those who should've been getting help, and those who were probably going to need help --"

"Let me guess," Manx grinned, "It came to 100%. "

"Well, close to it," Cole said.

"I've spent time in New York," Manx said, nodding, "I believe it."

"You were overwhelmed," Cole said to Reggie.

"I'm not sure that's the word," she said. "More like I felt I wasn't doing any good. It was like fighting a forest fire with a garden hose. What I liked about here when I came up for my interview, about the school, about Diamond Cove, was, like Dr. Manx said, a small school in a small town; I felt -- I *feel* -- like I can make a difference."

Manx nodded, appreciative, satisfied.

She looked to Cole. His smile was polite, but there was something in his look -- around the eyes -- where she knew he sensed there was more, maybe even that this wasn't the reason at all.

"Ahhh, another Diamond Cove newcomer!" and Manx nodded to the bar section of the restaurant. He was referring to the broad-shouldered man in a police uniform picking up a take-out food box at the bar. "Chief Petit!" Manx called and beckoned the policeman over.

Mid-30s, Regina guessed, with a tanned, mildly creased face that obviously loved the outdoors, hair short but not in a martial way as much as an easy-to-take-care of way, and while the uniform was comfortably loose, it couldn't conceal the fact that the gentleman took good care of himself. And while he smiled familiarly at Manx and Cole, there was something to it… Reggie had a sense there was a permanent tinge of melancholy to the man which, oddly, made the strong lines of his face more attractive.

"Dr. Manx," the officer said with a small, greeting smile, then to Cole, "Frank."

Reggie made a note: "Dr. Manx" vs. "Frank."

"Hello, Denny," Cole said, and Reggie saw something intangible pass between them; some kind of connection not shared with Manx.

"Regina," Manx went on, "this is Denny Petit, chief of what there is of the Diamond Cove Police Department. What is it, Denny? Three officers?"

"And a secretary," Petit shrugged in a way that said, But I'm happy with it.

"Denny's another recent transplant. Chicago, right?"

"Came out here just a few months ago. Same as these two guys. And this is…?" nodding at Reggie.

"Dr. Regina McLaren. She's taking the open seat for the department."

"Welcome to Diamond Cove," Petit said and took her hand, firmly but feeling no obligation to showboat his obvious muscles.

"Pleased to meet you, Chief."

"'Chief' feels a bit much for a crew of three."

"And a secretary," Reggie said, and they shared a grin. "In that case, Denny --"

"Regina?"

"My turn to say that feels a bit much. A little too regal for my tastes. My friends call me Reggie."

"It looks like you've made a new friend, Denny," Cole said. Was that approval in his voice?

Petit shrugged.

"Reggie here did some work with the New York Police Department," Cole added.

"Really?"

Reggie nodded it away. "It wasn't much. Some officers were referred to me who were having emotional problems. You were with a big city police department; I'm sure you know the kinds of things that came my way."

Petit nodded, but there was a sudden heaviness to him.

"I mention it," Cole said, "because I thought she might be of… Oh, that you two might have some interesting conversations, some common ground between two newbies."

An odd look went between Petit and Cole. Reggie felt Cole was giving a gentle push.

After a bit, Petit shrugged. "Maybe."

"Why don't you sit and have dinner with us?" Manx said.

Petit smiled his slightly melancholy smile and held up his take-out box.

"So, we get you a plate."

"Maybe another time." He turned to Reggie. "No offense?"

She nodded a no, but Cole had gotten her curious about the one man at the table who didn't seem to be vying for her attention. "Another time, then. Maybe we can have one of those 'interesting conversations'."

"Maybe," Petit said.

"Oh-oh." It was Cole. He was looking past Petit toward the door. "Maybe you should stick around, Denny. Your professional services might be required anon."

"I agree," Manx said glumly. "Dr. McLaren, you are about to see the liability of living in a small town with only one decent place to eat. All paths eventually cross here…however undesired that intersection might be."

Petit looked over his shoulder, his wide chest heaved in a silent sigh, and he pulled a chair up to the table. Reggie couldn't help but notice Petit made an extra effort to wedge his chair between Manx and Cole rather than to sidle up alongside her where there was ample room for another chair.

The three men were looking at the couple standing by the entrance at the "Wait to be seated" sign. Reggie glanced around and it seemed like everybody in the Clipper was looking in the same direction with expressions ranging from, "Oh, no, here we go again!" to, "Oh, this is gonna be good!"

They were middle-aged, but a battered middle age. Reggie had seen the same iconography in her office many times; a couple that had probably never belonged together, staying together in a poisonous brew of weakness, habit, and the angry frustration of feeling they had no place else to go.

They were also overdressed for the Clipper, for Diamond Cove in general in which, on campus and in town, Reggie had seen nothing -- with the exception of Jonathan Manx's garb -- that couldn't, at best, have passed as Business Casual back in New York. The woman had been handsome once, but now had a face saggy and creased from too much drink, too many cigarettes, and a decade or two of bitterness and anger. Her silver-gray hair had been poorly teased into a pouf that showed rather than hid its thinning. She wore a silvery cocktail dress matched by silvery high heels, too many rings, too-big earrings, a string of pearls, a shoulder wrap. She was ready for a night on a much bigger town than Diamond Cove.

The man, balding, a face permanently folded in resigned defeat, a sense amplified by his slumped shoulders, wore a tired-looking suit, carrying it with none of the aplomb of Jonathan Manx.

"Is she blind?" the woman said, making no effort at discretion, obviously meaning the hostess who was busy seating another party.

"She'll get to us," the man mumbled.

"In the meantime, let me numb the pain," and with that the woman abandoned the man for the bar. "Throw in an extra olive, honey," she told the bartender, and Reggie could hear from both her volume and the slight slur to her words that the woman had been primed before she'd shown up in the doorway of the Clipper, "because I'm hungry and that's the only thing in this hole fit to eat."

"Alan and Karen Danning," Manx said quietly to Reggie. "Living proof counseling doesn't help everybody. I've had a crack at them, so has Francis, so has everybody on the regular staff at the clinic."

Cole nodded his head helplessly. "I don't know why they even bother to come. I'm not sure they *want* things to get better. They fight you every step of the way. Either a neighbor or one of them has a complaint in to Denny - -. What, Denny, at least once a week?"

"At least," Petit said.

The hostess -- who took a second to steel herself, knowing what was coming -- put on a smile and led the Dannings to a booth. "Would you like menus?" the hostess asked.

"Why?" Karen Danning sneered, "Did something on them change in the last million years? And get me another one of these, missy," and she held up her empty martini glass.

"Think you could slow down just a tad?" Alan Danning asked quietly.

"Not really. Ok, missy, bring me a menu; I forget what flavors the swill comes in."

Reggie shook her head. She'd had troubled couples for clients, but nothing that fell into this kind of public outrageousness. She turned to Denny Petit. "And what part in this melodrama do you play?"

"We haven't gotten there yet, but if she keeps belting drinks back like that, it won't be long."

The hostess was back with Karen Danning's drink which she drained and then chomped down on the olive. "That takes care of dinner!"

"You wanted to come out for dinner," her husband said, "now you'll eat dinner!"

"I wanted to come out, so I didn't have to stay cooped up in the house staring at your sour puss for another night. How 'bout another one o' those for dessert, missy?"

"Bring her the chicken salad platter," her husband said, "and I'll have the roast beef. And no more drinks."

The hostess seemed relieved to have a reason to leave, but froze when --

"Where the hell're you goin', missy?" Karen Danning slurred. "This lump is my husband, not my boss. *I'll* decide when there's no more drinks and trust me, missy, we ain't there yet!"

"I said *enough*, Karen!" her husband snapped.

"Any second now," Manx said, and Reggie could sense Denny Petit getting ready to bolt from his chair.

Karen Danning had put on a face of mock surprise. "Good God, Alan, what's this? Could this be evidence of a spine? An honest to God backbone? Jesus Christ, lemme call the *AMA Journal*; it's a fucking medical miracle! Alan Danning has grown some *guts!* What's next, Alan? Raise your voice?" And then in an equally mocking sexy taunt, "Maybe put me across your knee for a good spanking? Hmmmm?"

"It never ceases to amaze me," her husband said, his face wrinkling in disgust, "how sickening you can get with so little effort."

"You need to unwind, hubby-wubby. How 'bout a drink?" And with that she emptied her water in her husband's lap, and while he was still reacting, tossed the glass at his head, narrowly missing.

"My cue," Denny Petit said. "Nice to meet you," he tossed over his shoulder at Reggie as he hurried over to the Dannings' table to referee them back into their chairs and make a strong recommendation that they ether quiet down or find another place to take their squabbling.

"I thought they were in particularly fine form tonight," Manx chuckled, "didn't you, Francis?"

But Francis Cole didn't seem amused. "I wish I could find the key," he said as much to himself as his tablemates. Then he looked over at Reggie, as if he'd suddenly realized he'd spoken aloud, and gave an embarrassed smile.

Reggie nodded that there was no need to apologize. "It's why we do what we do, isn't it?"

"That may be," said Manx, "but some things can't be fixed. Ahh, here comes dinner!"

Reggie was standing outside the Clipper with Manx and Cole. The sky was just turning a daunting royal purple, stars already beginning to pop up here and there with a clarity Reggie could never remember back in New York; every bit of sparkle standing out in a clear spoke.

"I still haven't gotten used to it," Cole said, quietly, as if in church. "They may be short on culinary choices up here, but it does have its compensations."

"Regina, you're missing the last act," Manx said, chortling. He was at the front window of the Clipper, apparently more enthralled at what was going on inside than the brilliance of a Maine evening.

Out of politeness more than curiosity, and mindful that Manx was her boss, Reggie turned to the window, Cole -- she felt for the same reason -- joining her.

After Denny Petit had read the Dannings the riot act, Alan Danning had tried to get his wife to join him in leaving, there'd been more -- and louder -- squabbling before the husband shook his head in surrender and stormed out. Karen Danning had cackled as if this was some kind of victory, then planted herself at the bar where she was now in sloppily coquettish conversation with a man ten years her junior clad in camouflage garb from head to toe.

It was clear the younger man's smile and attentiveness were less than sincere, and he made sure Karen Danning's glass was always full.

"Amazing," Manx said.

"Which one?" Cole said.

"Both. Someone should write a paper."

"What's amazing," Reggie said, "is how some men will put up with anything to sleep with anything."

Cole smiled wryly in agreement. "*Some* men."

"Gross generalizations are the bane of our profession," pronounced Manx. "Tsk-tsk. I have my car, Regina, can I drop you at the motel?"

"Actually, I've found a place. It's right on the cove, close enough to walk."

"She's renting from Anna Banana," Cole said. Then, to Reggie, "I'm sorry. That's what the students call her and I'm afraid I've picked up the habit." To Manx, "Ann Bonano's place."

"There was a notice on a bulletin board in the student center," Reggie explained.

Manx grinned. "I think you'll find it an interesting experience. She used to teach at the school, you know."

"So, she said. Art, wasn't it?"

"Which might explain things," Manx said. "You know; artists," which, as far as Reggie was concerned, didn't explain anything. "I'll see you in the office tomorrow morning and we'll get you settled in, work out schedules and such, brief you on the program, and get you ready for the start of the semester. It's week after next, but you'll be surprised, with syllabi, paperwork, and the like, how fast it'll be on us. Ciao!" and then Manx climbed into his old but well-kept Camry and drove off.

"When I moved up here, I asked if it was safe to be out at night," Cole said. "Philadelphia will do that to you. I imagine so will New York."

"And you were told?"

"I was told I'd have to pay somebody to mug me!"

They both laughed.

"Still," Cole went on, "and maybe it's just habit, but I'd feel better if I walked you home. I'm in that direction anyway."

The Clipper sat just off the crossroads that comprised all of downtown Diamond Cove. There was a two-floor sort-of mini department store at which, Cole explained, Reggie could find *anything* she needed in setting up a household. There was also a market, a bank, a couple of bars, a thrift store, a couple of craft shops, and a repair place that promised it could fix anything electronic from a toilet-drowned cell phone to a locked laptop.

One of the roads out of downtown led down to and around the head of the cove, paralleling the narrow pebble beach. They walked quietly, both enjoying the deepening sky that was turning into a blue-black blanket of diamond-like stars. The moon was full, incredibly bright, not dampened by smog or diluted by city lights. A moon glade cut across the cove looking solid enough to walk on. Wavelets across the cove picked up the moonlight and the entire inlet glittered.

It came to Reggie: "Diamond Cove."

"Diamond Cove," said Frank Cole, nodding in agreement and the same appreciation. Then, "Look who else is enjoying the evening."

The night sky was bright enough that Reggie had no problem identifying the man sitting on a cluster of weather-smoothed boulders near the water: Denny Petit. She could pick out the red glow of a cigarette in his hands.

"I thought we'd fixed that," Cole said as he and Reggie walked across the beach to Petit.

Petit was at first surprised by the voice, then turned, saw Cole, smiled with a bit of embarrassment as he looked at his cigarette, then flicked it out toward the low waves quietly lapping at the shore. "We had."

"We should talk about that sometime."

"I guess we should," Petit sighed.

"FYI Karen Danning is still at the Clipper. Looks like she's got some poor sap in her sights as a night cap."

Petit shrugged philosophically.

"Are you ok, Denny?" Cole asked, and, again, Reggie sensed something between the two men.

Petit shrugged again. "Just enjoying…" and he nodded out at the cove. "Chicago was never like this."

Cole nodded, they each said good night, and then he and Reggie continued on.

Reggie looked back at Petit growing smaller in the distance behind them. She smiled at Cole. "You're treating him!"

Now it was Cole's turn to smile, but sheepishly. "I've been trying to figure out how to bring it up without violating confidentiality. Inevitably, you'd bump into him at the clinic or my office, but I'm not sure I'd use the word 'treatment.' It's more like occasional conversations between friends, and I'm not putting it that way just to finesse the confidentiality issue; I like Denny, he's a good guy. But he does need someone to talk to. He needs something I can't give him; not professionally or even as a friend."

"You mean me. Because I did some work with the police back home."

"You'd know --"

Reggie was already shaking her head. "It was only a few officers, and it was hardly my strong suit. I don't know that I'd be of any more use than you."

"There's something else."

Reggie nodded for him to go ahead.

"You're new up here. I'm new up here. So is Denny and so is Jonathan. We could all use some friends. That even goes for Jonathan, even though he seems to be a world unto himself!"

Which was good for another laugh.

Reggie looked back along the beach where Denny Petit was now on his feet and heading in the other direction, crossing the road, and disappearing into the dark.

They continued along the curve of the beach until they reached a two-story house sitting atop a rocky rise. Like nearly every house in and around Diamond Cove, it was old –one hundred years, maybe more -- and also like most of the houses in the area, had an odd shapelessness to it, having been added onto haphazardly by one generation of resident or another, until it connected with what looked to have been a barn at one point.

Reggie and Frank Cole stopped at the foot of a flight of stone stairs leading up to the house.

"Well, here you are, delivered safe and sound," Cole said.

"Safe and sound."

They stood awkwardly for a second. Reggie wasn't sure if Cole was angling to continue the evening in some way, but she decided the matter with, "I guess I'll see you at school tomorrow."

"Tomorrow, then," he said, trying to find a gracious smile before turning and heading back along the beach.

"You should've kissed him," a voice came above.

Reggie looked up to one of the more recent additions to the house; a deck jutting out from what had once been the barn's loft. She saw a small head peeping over the edge of the deck, its wild curls haloing in the moonlight.

"It wasn't a date," Reggie said.

"Doesn't matter. A night like this should end with a kiss."

"Maybe *you* should've kissed him."

"I come after him, you'll see him doing the minute mile down that beach. If Jonny Manx hasn't stuffed you full of that snooty California wine he's always bragging about, c'mon up for a night cap."

The door to the house was unlocked -- it was always unlocked, something that left Manhattan-dwelling Reggie unnerved at night -- and then there was a narrow staircase of old, warped boards. At the top of the stairs, there was a door to her small apartment on the right, a door to the loft on the left.

The loft lights were out, but enough moonlight was coming through the several skylights that Reggie was able to navigate around a clutter of painter's easels, half-finished canvases and stacked blank ones, racks of paint. She found her way to the sliding glass doors which opened on the deck.

Ann Bonano was a spindly little thing, sixty-something or better, topped off with a spongy mop of gray hair. She was laying on one of two beach loungers and beckoned Reggie to its twin. Between them, in a pail filled with ice, was a cocktail shaker.

"Have a seat, have a drink," Ann offered, nodding at the unoccupied lounger.

"What're you drinking?"

"An old people's drink, I'm afraid; martinis."

"I could do a martini."

Ann reached down by the pail and came up with a martini glass. She threw an ice cube in the shallow bowl, swirled it around and then whipped the cube out into the night. "Your glass is now adequately chilled," she announced, and Reggie laughed. Ann poured a drink from the shaker, then reached down again to come up with a bottle of olives. "One or two?"

"I had a big meal," Reggie said.

"One, then," and she shook an olive out of the jar into the drink with a quiet little *blurp*. "Your drink, dear," and she offered up the glass with a bowed head. "Be careful with the glass. That's an honest-to-God martini glass. One of my few indulgences is nice glasses."

Reggie took the glass, took a sip, her head rocked back. "A might strong, isn't it?"

"And I thought you big city broads were supposed to be tough," Ann said. "I'm sorry I don't do Cosmos. You don't want it, fine, but don't throw it out. I'll finish it."

"Oh, I'll finish it," Reggie said.

"Was dinner that bad?"

"Not at all. Food wasn't bad and neither was the company."

"Was that the company I saw you with down there? From the school?"

"Frank Cole."

Ann nodded approvingly. "I was right; should've kissed him. He's a nice one."

"It wasn't a date, Ann."

"I know; the ritual welcome-to-the-school dinner at the Clipper. Who was the other guy? The one out on the beach? I've got a pretty good view of the whole shoreline from here."

"And good eyes, too. The police chief, Petit. Seems like a nice fella."

"I don't know him. But if you have to choose between Cole and Jonny Manx --"

"I'm not choosing anybody," Reggie said. "I just got here,"

"Well, sweets, it won't take you long to realize the pickin's up here is mighty slim. If you find one with all his teeth and a job, lasso him, brand him, and drag him home."

Reggie chuckled. "They told me you were a character."

"Did they?" She could see Ann grinning in the moonlight. She polished off her drink, splashed another into her glass, shook in a couple of olives. "I must've made quite an impression in the little time we were on campus together. They were just coming in while I was going out."

"Why did you leave?"

"I didn't leave, sweets. I was shit-canned."

"They didn't tell me that."

"Well, they're a diplomatic bunch."

They were quiet then. The view from the deck, thought Reggie, was even nicer than the view from the beach, and the soft sound of the small waves rolling in was lulling.

"Aren't you gonna ask me why I got canned?" Ann said, "Or are you a diplomatic type, too?"

"I didn't think it was necessarily any of my business."

"And you're supposed to be a shrink?"

"Ok," Reggie laughed, "why did they can you?"

"I'm an artist, sweets. They hired an artist to teach art which you'd think makes sense. But they *don't* want an artist to teach art because artists can't break art down into syllabi and learning outcomes and all that other institutional crap. Art ain't math."

"So, they had a problem with that."

"I think they had a bigger problem with me *telling* them they had a problem with that. In my own inimitable style."

"I'm getting a picture."

"I miss the paycheck, but maybe it was for the best. It was a bad fit. I hope you do better. Now I have a question for you, City Girl: what brought you up here?"

"Change of pace."

"That's all?"

Reggie beckoned at the panoramic moonlit seascape out in front of them. "Isn't that enough?"

"Believe it or not, it gets old after a while. Maybe a month or so and it'll be too damn cold for you to be out here enjoying it. And you haven't seen winter yet. And...I don't believe you."

Reggie was taken aback by the bluntness of it from a woman she hardly knew.

"Apologies," Ann said when she picked up on Reggie's reaction. "I was already two drinks in before you got here. I get a bit blabby by the third, and downright obnoxious after that."

"What about you?" Reggie countered. "I can't picture you having led a cloistered life loving only your art. Who did you rope, brand, and drag home?"

Ann smiled ruefully. "His alimony and your rent are keeping this place afloat. He didn't like artists either. Nice fella...but a bit of a dick."

"Then maybe you should make a run at Frank Cole? Or maybe Jonathan Manx?"

"Jonny Manx loves himself enough he doesn't need anyone else. And as for anybody else... No, City Girl, I've retired from the game. I leave it up to pretty young things like you, and you *are* a pretty young thing. If I played for the other team, I'd be tempted to give you a try myself. You'll do fine up here."

They grew quiet then, and as much as Ann Bonano had dismissed the routine beauty of Diamond Cove, she seemed to be enjoying the starry panorama as much as Reggie.

Reggie hadn't been aware her eyes were closing until Ann shook her by the arm. "You want me to just throw a blanket on you here?"

Reggie shook herself awake. "This concoction of yours is really hitting me." With great effort, she pulled herself to her feet. "I'll see you tomorrow, Ann.".

"By the way, I put a chain on your door. I knew you were uncomfortable with the open-door policy up here; I thought you might sleep better."

Reggie laughed. "Maybe you're right; us big city girls aren't that tough."

Between the full meal at the Clipper, Jonathan Manx's Russian River wine, and Ann Bonano's potent martinis, Reggie quickly fell into a deep, dreamless sleep for which she was grateful. Reggie was not particularly fond of her dreams.

But heavy as her sleep was, she had gotten used to middle-of-the-night calls during her practice in New York. That's when some of her clients -- especially those who were on the police force -- seemed most dogged by their demons, and she'd trained herself to drag herself to consciousness for a late-night call.

And that's what she did now. One hand blindly swept toward her night table trying to scoop up her phone while she babbled to no one in particular, "I'm up, I'm up, I'm up." She had the phone now, was still working mostly on automatic pilot: "Yeah, yes, hello, I'm up."

"Reggie?"

Her head was only moderately beginning to clear. "Who is this?"

"Denny Petit."

"Who?"

"Denny --. The police chief."

Reggie tried to rub the sleep out of her eyes, looked at the caller ID on her phone. It was, indeed, Denny Petit.

"I'm sorry to wake you but --"

"What time is it?"

"A little after six."

"I was going to have to get up soon any --" But now she began to pick up the somber tone in Petit's voice. "What's the matter?"

"I called Frank Cole first. He said I should call you. You know; because of your experience."

"My experience?"

"Back in New York. With the police."

Reggie felt a sickening, cold feeling in her stomach.

"I need your help, Reggie."

It took her a long moment before she said, unable to keep the sigh out of her voice, "Where are you?"

Chapter Two

It was, at first glance, a statelier house than most of those in town, with a colonnaded porch and lacking the usual slapdash add-ons. But the metal roof was spotted with rust, the paint on the walls weathered and cracking, the lawn unkempt. There were two patrol cars parked out front, a police officer by the front door, and Denny Petit waiting at the foot of the cracked cement walk.

"I hated doing this to you," he called across the road as Reggie climbed out of her car. "This is no way for anybody to start their day."

She shrugged it off as she crossed the road. She was close to saying the same thing to him. Back at her place, still half-asleep, she had crawled into baggy sweats, pushed her fingers through her bed-headed blonde hair, and hoped there'd be no children she'd frighten on the drive over. Petit was waiting for her with an outheld cup of coffee from the town's one Dunkin' Donuts.

"The least I can do," he said.

She smiled a thanks because, late August or not, the morning was chill, and her body wasn't quite awake. She took a sip, felt glad as it went down warming.

"Thing is," he began, looking away like an embarrassed schoolboy, "Frank Cole… Man, I knew he wanted us to talk, but I don't think this is what he had in mind."

"And just what is 'this'?"

Petit took a deep breath and nodded at the house. "Crime scene. Homicide."

Reggie found herself reflexively take a step backward. "Wait a second, I never worked --"

"I know, I know," Petit said. "Frank thought, well, because of your experience. With the police."

"That was *therapy*, not *forensics*." She pushed her coffee cup into one of Petit's hands and started back across the road to her car. "Thanks for the coffee."

"Please!"

The clear desperation in his voice stopped her even though it hadn't persuaded her.

"Look, Reggie, I was a good cop back in Chicago, but I was only ever a beat cop. I'm no detective. And this..." He shook his head. "It's already beyond me. I need help. Frank thought you were the closest thing to a, well, you get the picture."

She walked slowly back to him. "Do you have an ID on the victim?"

He nodded. "Karen Danning."

"Wasn't that the woman --"

"Making the scene at the Clipper last night? Yeah."

"Where's the husband?"

"We're trying to find him."

Reggie looked up the walk to the open door where the patrolman was standing and then back to Petit. True, she hadn't done forensic work, hadn't worked crime scenes, but she'd dealt with enough traumatized police officers to be less than enthusiastic about going through that front door. Then she looked to Petit. Those two, soft brown orbs were not a hard cop's eyes, and maybe in that softness she was getting a feeling about why he'd left Chicago.

She couldn't get herself to say a "yes" aloud, but took back her cup of coffee, nodded, and followed Petit up the walk. "How'd you find her?"

"Paper boy. Saw the door open, went inside… If you're looking for psych patients, I have a feeling that kid's going to need some treatment after what he saw." Petit stopped at the door, nodded to the young patrolman trying to affect a look of professional cool without much luck. "This is Officer Cooney --"

"Carney, Chief," the patrolman corrected.

"I'm still getting the names down," Petit said to Reggie. "You said you never dealt with crime scenes?"

"I dealt with policemen. Not police work."

"I've seen a lot and I still think this is pretty bad. I don't know how, but you should prepare yourself."

They stepped through the door, past a small entry foyer into a living room. It had been nice furniture once, modern once, but now well past a date with the curb. And there was a smell, heavy enough to cut through the mustiness of the place to set her wincing. "Who puked?"

"One of my other cops." He turned to Carney. "What's his name? Mooney? Monday?"

"Mondry, Chief. He's out back, getting some air."

"My cops haven't ever dealt with a violent crime scene either," Petit explained to Reggie. "She's over here behind the sofa."

Reggie followed slowly. Coming into view was a set of bare feet, toenails painted a garish red, then…a blanket.

"Hey, Clooney!" Petit called.

"Carney," Reggie corrected.

"Right here, Chief."

"Who put the blanket over her?"

"Me, Sir. You saw how she --"

"Yeah, 'Me, Sir,' I saw. But did you ever hear of protecting the integrity of the crime scene?"

Carney's lips pursed into a silent, "Oh."

"Front seat of my car. There's a camera and a recorder. Go fetch." As Carney jogged off, Petit bent over to grab the edge of the blanket. He looked over at Reggie.

She could already feel the coffee churning in her stomach as she nodded.

Petit pulled the blanket away.

Reggie got a quick glance of a silvery silky bathrobe, drenched with blood up by the open neck, and then under the tangled hair, where Karen Danning's face should've been, a mass of red pulp. She dropped her coffee, turned away, grabbed for something to hold her up as her head went spinning.

Then Petit was there, holding her. "It's ok. Why don't you go outside?"

She shook her head no. "Sorry about the coffee. Integrity of the crime scene."

He gave her a small smile. "It's ok. I'll make a note. Be careful what you touch; I haven't printed anything yet."

Carney was back, handed the camera and recorder over to Petit and then took his post back at the door. Outside, Reggie could see a small crowd gathering at the foot of the walk, necks craning to try to get a glimpse into the house. People are the same all over, she thought. And then it occurred to her the body by the sofa testified to that very same unfortunate commonality in human nature.

"Why don't you stay here," Petit said. "I can talk this through."

She nodded. She heard him kneel down by the body, the snap and crackle of him wrestling on a pair of vinyl gloves, the click of the recorder being switched on, saw the occasional flash of his camera as he took photos of the scene.

"Hm. Still has her earrings, wedding ring, decent-looking rock, too. Purse on the sofa. Wallet's still here, credit cards…"

"So not a robbery."

"It looks like there was one blow to the back of the head. I figure the perp blitzes her from behind. She goes down. The blood pattern on the floor suggests he rolled her over on to her back, and then the rest."

"Wait, she was already down when…well, when the rest…?"

"Looks like."

"How bad is the wound at the back of her head?"

"I'd be surprised if that didn't kill her right off. Looks like a deep penetration through the skull. Maybe the perp didn't know she was dead, so…"

Reggie risked another quick glance at the body, at the savaged face before quickly turning away. "No. He knew. This was rage."

The sofa faced a fireplace. Reggie saw a line of framed photographs propped up on the mantlepiece. She walked to the fireplace, careful not to look down where Petit was still kneeling by Karen Danning's bloodied corpse.

"No blood under her fingernails, no bruising, no defensive wounds, no signs of a struggle. She's about an hour or two into rigor, maybe a little more, puts time of death somewhere between ten and twelve. We checked the doors and windows: no signs of forced entry."

"That doesn't mean anything. People around here don't lock their doors."

"They will now. It was somebody she was comfortable enough to let get close enough to blindside her, she's wearing a robe and nothing underneath… After what we saw last night at the Clipper… You think the husband?"

Reggie was studying the pictures, trying not let the speckles of sprayed blood across the smiling faces distract her. Karen Danning and her husband in younger and happier days; the young Dannings with a small, pretty, dark-haired, big-eyed girl, maybe ten; then what Reggie guessed was the same girl as a teenager; then the same girl a little older in a simple wedding dress with a young man about the same age in an ill-fitting tux; then the girl with the man and a baby; then the girl alone with a young boy with his mother's dark hair and equally dark eyes. In that last picture, the girl seemed to be forcing a smile, and the boy was stone-faced.

"I said, what about the husband?" Petit pushed.

"I don't know. I got the impression they'd been living that way a long time."

"Maybe it was one argument too many."

"Maybe. Who's this in these pictures? I recognize the husband."

"I'm told there's a daughter. Hey, Clancy!"

"Carney," the officer said as he stepped into the room but stayed clear of the area around the sofa.

"Didn't you tell me the Dannings had a daughter?"

"Yeah, she lives over on Ridgewood with her kid."

"She's married?" Reggie asked.

"Was. Divorced. Two years ago, I think."

"How do you know all this?" Petit asked,

"Small town, Chief."

"Keep that in mind if you consider misbehaving," Petit warned Reggie. "She been notified?" he asked Carney.

"Not yet. I --. Well, none of us knew, um --"

"Yeah, I know, above your pay grade. You can go back on the door and would you tell those people out there to please stay the hell off the property? You know; crime scene and all that?"

"Sorry, Chief, I'm on it."

With a long, deep sigh, Petit rose from the body.

Reggie turned away from the photos toward Petit. There was a certain... Was it despair on his face? "Are *you* alright?"

He smiled ruefully. "I took this job because they told me this kind of thing didn't happen here." Then the smile evaporated, and he seemed to be sinking into some darker place.

Reggie sought to pull him out of it: "Any idea on the murder weapon?"

"Hm?"

"Murder weapon."

He beckoned Reggie to follow him, pointing to a trail of dark red spots on the floor leading to the back of the house. Reggie followed Petit into a kitchen that must've been impressive when it had been redone twenty or so years before, but the edges of cabinets were chipped, drawers didn't shut, and apparently no one in the house was a bug about washing dishes. Petit pointed to the kitchen sink.

Among the stacked dirty dishes was a hammer, the kind with a ball at the back end rather than a claw. The ball was shiny with blood mingled with hair and what Reggie guessed were bits of tissue. The hammer lay in a pool of blood.

"What do you call that kind of hammer?" Reggie asked. "A ball something?"

"Ball peen, as opposed to a claw hammer."

"Why the ball? What do you use those for?"

"You mean besides caving in someone's skull? Metalwork, I think."

Reggie considered the unkempt house, her admittedly brief but memorable viewing of the cowed Mr. Danning the night before. "Is there a basement?"

Petit pointed to a door off the kitchen. "Wait." Petit used a pen to flick the basement light on. "I told you; I haven't printed anything yet."

Reggie nodded, went down creaking stairs. The basement showed the house's true age… rough stone walls, musty smell, damp. It was a cluttered space; junk accrued by the Dannings over decades together that no one bothered to throw out: old clothes, odd chairs, broken suitcases, stuffed cardboard boxes splitting at their corners. But Reggie didn't find what she was looking for. "How about a garage?"

"This way," Petit said, clearly curious. He led her back upstairs, out the back door into the yard where another young policeman -- the aforementioned Mondry, Reggie assumed -- was sitting on the ground, ashen, still not having recovered from the grisly sight inside.

The garage door was open. More clutter, garbage cans, broken-toothed rake, lawn mower that looked like it hadn't been moved in years. No car.

"The husband left her at the Clipper, took the car, Petit said. "I'm waiting to hear back from the Bureau of Motor Vehicles for tag numbers, make and model."

"How'd she get home?"

"Good question. But you didn't come out here because you didn't find the car in the cellar. What've you been looking for?"

"Workshop. Workbench. *Tools*. Mr. Danning didn't come off to me as a do-it-yourselfer. What time were you refereeing the Dannings at the Clipper last night?"

"I usually pick up dinner between six and seven. So sometime after six."

"If I had doubts about the husband before, I'm pretty sure now, unless there was some place he could swing by to buy himself a hammer after he left."

"There's a hardware place just outside of town but that would've been way out of his way. That kind-of-a-department-store, but they close at six on weeknights."

"If this was on impulse, the killer would've used something at hand, something familiar...or something he brought with him."

"Or with *her*."

"Or her. "

"Let's check the rest of the house."

The only room of interest was the bedroom, furnished with a bedroom set too ornate and bulky for the small space.

Petit had his recorder on, again. "Two liquor glasses on the night table, one showing lipstick, the dress she was wearing last night on the floor but not torn. Possible semen stains on the sheets."

"She was talking to someone at the bar when I left," Reggie said, "and I don't think they were just passing the time."

Petit was standing with Carney, shaking his head over the crowd at the roadside which had continued to grow. "Jesus, we should sell tickets," Petit said to no one in particular, then he seemed to remember Reggie was there and smiled apologetically. "Something else I never got used to." He turned back to Carney. "Who's the kid out back with the weak stomach?"

"Mondry, Chief."

"Tell Mondry to go wake up the manager of the Clipper, run down whoever was tending bar last night and see if maybe he or she knows who was schmoozing with Karen Danning. You wait here for the -- What do we have? A coroner? A medical examiner?"

"I don't know. We never needed one. I guess they'd do the autopsy at the county hospital."

Petit turned to Reggie shaking his head. "Sometimes I do miss Chicago." Then back to Carney. "Notify them to come for the body. Meantime, seal this place but good and *don't* touch *anything.* Don't use the bathroom, don't get a drink of water, keep your damn hands in your damn pockets whenever you're in the house, got it? When the wagon gets here, ride in with the body, tell whoever does the autopsy to specifically look to see if Karen Danning had had sexual relations recently, and to get a DNA sample if she had and her guest left a calling card."

"Ew," Carney said, and Reggie tried to hide a smile.

"Well, yeah, police work does sometimes include a degree of 'ew'. Live with it." To Reggie: "I was never good at this part. Would you mind coming along? Your professional assistance would be appreciated."

Reggie nodded and headed for her car. "I'll drive if you want."

"Where are you going?" Carney called after them.

"Somebody has to tell the daughter," Petit called back. "You want to do it?"

Carney made another "Ew" face.

"Yeah, I didn't think so."

Reggie drove according to the brief directions Petit had given her; it never took much time to drive anywhere in Diamond Cove. She heard a long, heavy exhalation from the passenger side and glanced over to see Petit slumped in his seat, elbow parked on the arm rest and his chin on his fist.

"You ok?" she asked.

"The year before I left Chicago there were almost thirty thousand violent crimes in that city. Murder, assault, rape… I could populate Diamond Cove five, ten times over with those victims."

"That's why you left."

"You feel helpless. No matter how many perps you bust, it's the same shit every day, every year. Oh, sorry, pardon my language."

Reggie laughed. "I've heard worse."

It was Petit's turn to chuckle. She thought it made a nice, warm sound, liked the way the lines around his mouth deepened when he smiled; it pushed off the heaviness that seemed to always hang on him.

"I'll bet you have," he said, and then without the smile, "I'll bet you have."

There were no apartment buildings as such in Diamond Cove. Instead, there were old rooming houses and homes which had been expanded and converted into apartments. It was one of the latter where Marcia Danning lived. It had been quite the private home in its days; a wide, covered porch, large windows downstairs, a fair bit of land. But most of the property was now a parking lot for tenants, and after counting the eight mailboxes crowded alongside the double front doors, Reggie couldn't believe that so many apartments had been squeezed into the house's two floors.

She and Denny Petit sat in her car across from the house for a while, Reggie waiting for Petit to make the first move.

Then, from Petit, a sighed, "God, I hate this."

Reggie began to get the feeling he'd sit there forever if she didn't prod him somehow. "Whenever you're ready," she said after a bit.

He smiled at her, sadly, knowing what she was doing. "Yeah." He slowly climbed out of the car, she followed him across the front yard, up the stairs to the porch. There was a door buzzer button by each mailbox.

"Marcia Danning," Reggie read on the name taped to one mailbox. "She went back to her maiden name."

Petit rang the buzzer, and a woman's voice came from above: "Who is it?"

They peeped out from under the porch roof and saw Marcia Danning -- Reggie recognized her from the mantlepiece photos -- with her head hanging outside a second-floor window. From the look on the woman's face, Reggie could tell she didn't know what to make of the two people below: the man in uniform paired with the stray-haired woman in rumpled sweats.

"Police, Miss Danning," Denny explained. "Can we come up and talk to you?"

"This isn't about my son, is it? You should talk to Suzy Innis's kid first because it was his idea."

"No, it's about your mother."

Which only seemed to puzzle her more.

"Please, Miss Danning, it's important."

"Wait there. I have to let you in."

A moment later and they could hear shuffling on the other side of the door and then the *thunk* of a dead bolt getting thrown, and the door opened a crack. The most recent pictures on the mantlepiece must've been taken some time ago, Reggie thought. This Marcia Danning was in her early thirties, not unattractive if she hadn't had the worn look of someone with too many worries and not enough hours in the day to get done what she needed to do.

"You said this was about my mother?"

"Can we come in?" Pettit asked.

"Look, I'm trying to get my son off to school, I have to get to work --"

"You might want to hold off on sending your son out," Reggie said.

Marcia Danning's face wrinkled into a curious frown. "Who're you?"

"She's with me, Miss Danning," Petit said. "I thought she might help."

More curious, more frowning. "Help with what?"

"We really should talk inside," Reggie said.

At some point, Reggie could see, the alarm bells were going off for Marcia Danning. She nodded reluctantly, let the door swing open. "Up the stairs, you'll see the open door."

Reggie followed Petit up the stairs. The apartment inside the open door was a cramped few rooms.

Breakfast dishes were still on the table in the eat-in kitchen, and a surly teen with hair drifting down over his face, maybe fourteen or so -- Reggie recognized him as a slightly older version of the young stone-faced boy from the mantlepiece photos -- was stretched out on a fold-out sofa bed in what Reggie guessed was supposed to be a living room, TV remote in his hand, listlessly flipping through TV channels. Amid the breakfast clutter on the table Reggie also noticed a few textbooks heavily fringed with place-marking sticky notes. She looked from the TV-locked teen to the books, thinking all those place markers seemed uncharacteristically diligent.

"David!" his mother snapped. "I told you to get ready!"

"I'm waiting for you," he mumbled, barely moving his lips.

"We should talk to you alone," Reggie said.

"I thought you told me not to let him go to school."

"We should talk to you first," Reggie said.

The frown and the curiosity began to melt into alarm. "David, go wait for me on the porch."

"I'm watchin' this," he mumbled and gave a little wave of the TV remote.

"David!"

"Jesus Christ, Mom!" he snapped, tossed the remote down and stormed out of the apartment.

No look of apology from Marcia Danning, no self-consciousness, no defensiveness, just a glare at Reggie and Petit and a sharp, "What?"

"You look like you have your hands full," Reggie said, careful not to sound judgmental.

"He's a teen. Were you an angel when you were a teen?"

"Hardly," Reggie said.

"I mean, yeah, he does run my ass ragged," the woman said as she went into the other room to turn off the blaring TV.

"You better sit down, Miss Danning," Petit said and pulled out one of the mismatched kitchen table chairs.

With a wary look, Marcia Danning took a seat. "My mother get into another brawl with her husband?"

She didn't say, "My father," Reggie noted.

"Actually, we're not sure. Well..." Petit clearly didn't know how to break the news.

Reggie pulled another chair up close to Marcia Danning, set a hand on her knee. "The thing is, Miss Danning, your mother's dead."

It was a curious reaction, Reggie thought. The woman nodded, frowned as if contemplating something deeply. Then, "Well you wouldn't be here if she had a heart attack or something," and she looked to Petit.

"It appears she was murdered."

Again, no obvious reaction, just some nodding as if she were agreeing with something she was saying to herself. Then, "Do you think it was her husband?"

There it is, again, Reggie thought. "Don't you mean your father?"

Marcia Danning pushed back from the table and began to walk restlessly in the little open space there was in the kitchen and living room. "That...*man* is not my father. My father died when I was five. Car accident. He'd been drinking. If you knew my mother, you'd know why. My mother married…*Alan*…I was still a kid. I think I was ten, twelve, I don't remember exactly. But he is *not* my father!"

She remembers how old she was when her father died, Reggie noted, but the vagueness of her mother marrying her second husband, the angry edge to her voice when she referred to him…

"Do you know where he might be?" Petit asked.

"She doesn't," Reggie said, and that froze the pacing woman in her tracks. "You haven't talked to them in some time, am I right?"

Surprised but curious, Marcia Danning nodded. "How did you -- …" But then she shook her head, passing it off.

She doesn't want to go there, Reggie thought. Marcia turned to Petit. "So; do you think it was Alan?"

"We don't know anything yet, Miss Danning. Our first step is to try to get everybody who could possibly be involved to account for themselves last night."

"Last night? That's when it happened?"

"Late last night. The body wasn't discovered until this morning."

She grinned wickedly, anticipating: "Last night I was working at the college library. I'm there three nights a week."

"Can anybody verify that?"

"Let me save you a little effort, um --"

"Chief Petit."

"I was at the library 'til ten. I've got my supervisor and anybody who checked out a book last night to tell you where I was. And, no --" and here she turned toward

Reggie, "– I'm not all that broken up about it. And, yes, if I'd had the chance and the nerve, I might've considered doing it myself."

Reggie had to smile at the woman's forthrightness. But in Reggie's experience, that kind of armor was often a hard scar over a deep wound.

"What about after ten?" Petit asked.

"I walked home."

"Long way from the school, isn't it?"

"About two miles. I don't mind. It's the only time I get to myself."

Reggie looked around the cramped, disheveled apartment. I understand, she thought.

"Anybody see you on your walk?" Petit asked.

"Not a goddamn soul," and she held out her wrists as if waiting to be handcuffed.

"What do you do with your son when you're working?"

"Sometimes he stays with friends. Sometimes he hangs out here. Oh, maybe *he* did it!" When she saw no one smiling, "I was joking."

"We need someone to come down to County General and formally identify the body."

A beat, then, "Let me get my coat."

"It's not very pretty," Petit warned.

"I lived with that woman for sixteen years, mister. Neither was that."

"What about David?" Reggie asked. "Do you think you should tell him first?"

Marcia Danning went to the kitchen window, looked down at where Reggie guessed her son was hanging out on the front porch. She shook her head. "Later. If I could get away with it, I'd never tell him. In fact, I wish he'd never known she was still alive."

Reggie set a coffee down in front of Marcia Danning, then sat across from her at the table in a far corner of the hospital cafeteria. Marcia had come out of the morgue pale and shaken, and she didn't look much better now. She still seemed dazed, taking a moment to become aware of the cup in front of her. She shook her head as if coming awake. "Thanks," she mumbled, and took a sip. "Ech, that's not the stuff to settle your stomach."

"Would you like me to get you something else?"

Marcia shook her head. "Well, he warned me it wouldn't be pretty."

"I'm sorry you had to go through this. Where's your son? David, is it?"

"Home. I wouldn't have wanted him to see this."

"How'd he take the news?"

Marcia looked out the large windows of the cafeteria at the woods around the hospital, just starting to show the earliest tinges of their autumnal colors. She looked here and there, as if trying to find the answer to a puzzle, before she turned back to Reggie, cocked her head, puzzle unsolved. "I was kinda surprised. He was really broken up."

"That's only natural. She was his grandmother."

"I left home when I was sixteen. David knew *about* her, but he'd never met her. In a town this small, that's not easy."

Remembering the photos of Marcia and David on Karen Danning's mantlepiece, Reggie was puzzled, too. "Why did you leave home?"

Marcia seemed to pull into herself, lock her eyes on her coffee. "I really don't feel like doing a Q & A just now, do you mind?"

Someone nearby uttered an apologetic, "Um," and both women turned to find Denny Petit standing a few steps off, a manila envelope in his hand. "Miss Danning, again, I'm sorry for your loss. You'll be notified as soon as the body is released."

Marcia Danning's face went hard. "Notified to do *what?*"

"Well, um, any arrangements you may want to make --"

She abruptly stood up. "Talk to Alan. He was her husband, let him deal with it." She glanced quickly at her phone for the time. "David can skip school, but I can't afford to skip work."

"We may have to talk --"

She brushed by Petit. "You know where I am," she called back as she hurried out of the cafeteria.

Petit took her seat across from Reggie, his eyes locked on the cafeteria doors still swinging shut after Marcia Danning. "What do you think?"

"About what?" Reggie asked.

Petit nodded in the direction of the disappeared Marcia. "She seems like another candidate to me."

Reggie toyed meditatively with her coffee cup. "If I'm reading things right, if she was going to kill anybody,

I think it'd be Alan Danning." She saw the question in Denny Petit's face. "I've seen similar signs before."

Petit's face sagged with realization. "You think he --"

"I don't *know*, but, like I said, I've seen the signs before."

Then his face clouded, twisted in an anger Reggie hadn't seen on him before, that she would have thought out of character. "That son of a bitch," he hissed.

"Denny, it's a supposition, not a fact."

He took a deep breath, seemed to be trying to rein himself in.

"There's something else," Reggie said and told him about what Marcia had said about having avoided her mother since she'd left home, and how that was contradicted by the photos at the Danning house.

"She could be lying."

"I don't think so," Reggie said. "That'd be too easy a lie to catch. What's in the envelope?"

"Coroner's preliminary notes from the post. Some interesting stuff. Karen Danning had had sexual relations that night, but they don't appear to have been forcible."

There was a sense of incompletion in his voice. "But?"

And now he looked away. My God, Reggie thought, he's *blushing*.

"I didn't grow up in a convent, Denny. If you're embarrassed, you can close your eyes while you tell me."

He cleared his throat and made an obvious effort to appear coolly professional. It was hard for Reggie not to smile at the transparency of the act.

"It would appear," Denny began, "that whatever went on in Karen Danning's bedroom got, well, um…"

"Hot and heavy?"

Denny winced even as he nodded in agreement. "Here, why don't you just read the damn thing yourself," and he handed over the envelope.

Reggie scanned the scrawled notes quickly. "So, this is talking about love bites and small bruises, like from a hard pinch, on her breasts, buttocks, back of the neck. She liked it rough." She looked up, smiled again at the red-faced police chief looking at the ceiling, out the window, anywhere but at Reggie. "Big tough Chicago cop," she poked. "What were you out there? A crossing guard?"

"I wish," he said, and she thought that a curious remark. "You were right about that idea of rage. Doc says she was dead from the first hit."

"The one to the back of the head."

He nodded. "Says it's hard to tell, but she may have been hit in the face twenty, twenty-five times after that."

"Jesus…" Then she noticed a clock on the cafeteria wall. "Damn. Marcia Danning isn't the only one who has to get to work. I can drop you at the station; it's on the way."

"Actually," and he was looking at his phone in answer to a text alert, "you might want to come in with me."

"Denny, another time. I'm running *really* late --"

"You might want to be there for this, Reggie. It looks like we've got Karen Danning's love biter."

The municipal building was a small, red brick building looking like a cross between a church and a small-town schoolhouse. All the municipal offices -- mayor's office, public works, etc. -- were housed in the one building. There was a side door marked "Police," and Reggie followed Petit on through. Inside, at the front desk, was a small slip of a woman with tangled gray hair and a wrinkled face which looked permanently unperturbed.

"Grace Whitney," Petit introduced, "this is --"

"Dr. Regina McLaren," Grace said without looking up from the paperwork she was busy with. "She's the new shrink at the school."

Petit turned to a surprised Reggie. "Small town," he explained.

"I thought they dressed more stylish in Manhattan," Grace said, again without looking up.

"It's a new look."

Grace shrugged. She nodded at the door marked, "Chief." "He's in there waiting for you. Came in about 20 minutes ago. Says soon's he heard about Karen Danning, figured you'd be wanting to talk to him."

Pettit headed for the door, Reggie following.

"Make sure you ask him his name," Grace said, and Reggie couldn't be sure, but it looked like the corner of the woman's pursed mouth twitched in what might possibly have been a smile.

Inside the small office, sitting at a chair in front of Petit's desk was the young man Reggie recognized from the Clipper, still in his camos. Reggie wondered if it was the same outfit from the night before or if the man's wardrobe was just a series of camouflage outfits.

The man seemed to hardly notice Petit as the chief took his seat behind his desk. Instead, he seemed to be trying to figure out the meaning of the young woman in sweats with barely combed hair.

Petit set a legal pad in front of him, grabbed a pencil from a cup full of them on his desk. "So, Mr. --?"

"O'Toole."

"First name?"

The man hesitated.

"First name?"

The man took a breath. "Peter."

Petit put his pencil down. Reggie grinned.

"Peter O'Toole?" Petit said.

The man winced and nodded. Clearly, he'd been through this before. "My mom was a fan o' the guy, whaddaya want from me? She musta seen all his movies a million times."

Petit fought his own grin, picked up his pencil. "Ok, Mr. --. Ok. You have something to say about Karen Danning's death?"

"Well, yeah. I was, um…"

"You were with her last night," Reggie put in. "I saw you two at the bar at the Clipper."

O'Toole frowned at Reggie. "Who's she?" he asked Petit.

"She's consulting on the case." He looked over at Reggie to see if she was ok with that description. Reggie gave an I'm-flattered nod.

"I mean, uh, does she, you know, have to be *here?*"

"What's the problem?" asked Petit.

Reggie held up a finger to Petit; let me take this. She stood behind O'Toole, where he wouldn't have to look her in the eye. "You went home with her, didn't you?"

A bit shame-facedly, O'Toole nodded. "Well, let's say I takes her home. She don't have a ride, so I gives her a lift in my truck."

"That's all?" Reggie said. "Just a ride? You two had seemed pretty friendly at the bar."

"Well, you know, we have a few, right? You know how it is."

"*I* don't know," Petit pressed.

"She came on to you," Reggie offered.

"I guess that's a way to put it."

"Ok," Petit said, "you took her home, you went inside, right? Everybody's had a few, romance is in the air, you wind up in the bedroom."

"Anyways, here's the thing…"

"Yes?"

"'Cause I figger you're gonna see some stuff 'n' I don't want nobody gettin' a wrong idea 'cause a how she ended up."

"We're listening."

O'Toole took a deep breath. "It's not like I'm a prude or nothin'…"

"Hey, Lawrence of Arabia, just spill it."

"Who's he?"

Petit and Reggie exchanged a small grin and a headshake. She held up a finger again.

"Let me help you out, Peter."

"Pete."

"Fine, Pete. She liked it a little rough."

O'Toole nodded. "Thing is, she keeps, you know, she wants me to -- … She wants it even rougher."

"How rough?" Petit asked.

"She starts wantin' me to slap her around. I mean she's flat out sayin', 'Hurt me, hurt me,' 'n' stuff like that. So, ok, I'm thinkin' this is too weird even for me. Husband comes home, sees her all banged up, somebody's gonna call a cop, how'm I gonna look? So…"

"So, you left."

"Pete-boy, I says to myself, this ain't goin' nowhere good."

"What time did you leave?"

"You think I was lookin' at clocks, Chief?"

"You see anybody hanging around her house when you left?"

"I wasn't lookin' but I 'member the street bein' empty. I know you're new here, Chief, but you know this place is a ghost town come ten o'clock 'n' it was a helluva lot later 'n' that when I lit out."

"Ok, Pete, we're going to take a mouth swab for DNA in case you weren't the only one who left something behind. Then make sure you leave your contact information with Grace in case we need to talk to you, again."

After they were done with O'Toole, Petit walked Reggie back to her car.

"I assume you're not seriously considering young Mr. O'Toole," Reggie said.

"I'm not ruling anything out, but he's definitely not a strong contender. Look, Reggie, would you mind…?"

They were stopped at her car. She had to smile; broad shoulders, outdoorsy face, a boxer's hands, but he managed to look like a teenager walking a girl home from school for the first time. "Go ahead and ask."

"I just don't want you to take this the wrong way."

"Go-ahead-and-ask."

"This thing's really got me beat. I was wondering – only if you had the time – if we could, you know, sit together some time and talk this thing through."

"Maybe over dinner?"

"Doesn't have to be dinner. Coffee, something."

"Dinner's fine."

"Well, then," and he smiled and opened her car door for her.

"Well, then," and she beamed him one right back before she climbed in her car and headed off toward the university.

Chapter Three

Frank Cole met Reggie in the campus's main parking lot. When she saw the look on Cole's face at her appearance, she began tugging at her sweats as if that could somehow make them fit less like sweats. She ran her fingers through her hair although she doubted it would do much good.

"I'm sorry," she said, "but I've been with Denny all morning on this Danning thing and haven't had --, well, I probably should've gone home first before --"

Cole waved away her concerns. "Around here that passes for semi-formal."

"I hate going to see Dr. Manx like this."

"You look fine." Cole grimaced. "Oh, God, that sounded like a line, didn't it?"

"A little bit."

"I better show you your office before I get my *other* foot in my mouth!"

As they walked across the small campus -- many of its buildings being converted Victorian era homes separated by grassy squares where students, already arriving on campus, gathered in chatty clumps, or tossed Frisbees and Nerf footballs back and forth -- Reggie was struck by how many seemed to know Cole, waving and calling out, "Hey, Doctor Frank!"

"You've made quite a few connections for someone who hasn't been here very long," Reggie observed, impressed.

"They were students here for the summer session and early orientation. It's easy to feel for them, especially the freshmen: lonely, isolated, some of them can't afford cars so on top of everything else they feel stranded. Most of them are first generation college, so the parents don't always realize how much their kids still need them. Hey, Andy!"

They were passing a quad around which were arranged several low, porticoed brick buildings: dorms. Cole was waving to a pudgy young man, eighteen or nineteen, long hair hanging down over his face, who was unloading some trash bags loaded with his belongings from the back of a mud-splattered, rust-spotted old SUV. The couple Reggie assumed were his parents -- a frumpy, prematurely aged woman and a burly, beer-bellied man in a plaid jacket and baseball cap -- stood nearby.

Reggie had heard the father before Cole had called out, constantly nettling the boy: "Watch how ya handle those, ya gonna tear 'em 'n' yer crap's gonna be all over the street 'n' then what?"

At Cole's greeting, the boy looked up, at first smiled, then at his father's, "Who's this guy?", seemed to shrink a bit, and give half-hearted wave back.

Cole steered Reggie away from the family. "Best leave them be."

As they walked away, Reggie empathetically winced as she heard the father: "You think you're gonna get anywhere treatin' these muckety-muck professors like that?"

Cole led them into another brick building, one of the newer structures on the campus, with a sign by the door: "Computer Sciences." Inside, Reggie followed Cole down a staircase to a dark hallway lined with office doors. Cole stopped at a door marked, "Dr. R. McLaren," and swung the door open.

"Jesus," she said, "it looks like a cell!"

Cole laughed but she wasn't wrong: glazed cinder block walls, a few small windows high up on the outside wall where she could see sneakered and sandaled feet go by, a gray metal desk, an empty gray metal bookcase.

"Not quite as cozy as your New York digs?" Cole joked. "It's only temporary, at least that's what Jonathan says. We're a new department so they squeezed us in where they had room. Jonathan's hoping to have us out of this dungeon by the spring semester. I just want to check my schedule before we head over to meet with his imperial majesty."

Cole's office was two doors down. He unlocked his door, went to his desk to flip through a desktop calendar.

"You've set yours up quite nicely!" Reggie commented. Cole had floral curtains over the small windows, the walls broken up with landscape prints, bits of souvenir and junk shop bric-a-brac interspersed with the books on his bookshelves, a mini fridge tucked in the corner, a living room chair in another corner for visitors.

"I spend more time here than my apartment, so why not make it homey?" Cole said. "Besides, it helps the kids when they come in to see me." He offered her a small Perrier from the fridge, gestured her to the guest chair.

"Shouldn't we be getting over to the boss?"

"He'll wait. I wanted to ask you how it's going with Denny Petit?"

"Fine. He wants to meet to talk over the case. He says he's in over his head."

Cole leaned back in his desk chair, pursed his lips in a wry face. "He says."

"You think he has ulterior motives?" she joked.

"Be careful."

"Why?"

"Did Denny say anything about why he left Chicago?"

"Not directly. I got the feeling it was a typical case of burn-out. God knows I saw enough of it down my way."

"No doubt that's part of it, but that's not why he left. He was made to resign."

"Oh?" Reggie felt an unpleasant tingle at the back of her neck.

"Domestic call. Husband beating his wife. I guess it was one call too many. Denny put the man in the hospital. He was told if he resigned, there'd be no charges."

"This is why you've been pushing us to chat."

"I thought, because of your experience --"

"Because of my experience, I'm not the person who can help him."

"I don't --"

She set her unfinished Perrier bottle down on a nearby bookshelf with finality. "Let's go see the boss."

They met Manx in a conference room over at the campus library. Manx told them how proud the school was of the library. It had only opened just a few years before, had state of the art audio/video equipment and computer resources, and at four stories, was the tallest building on the grounds; in fact, it was, one of the tallest in all of Diamond Cove.

Manx had cued up a DVD hooked to the room's built-in projection system. "Your class work will be pretty routine. There's a master syllabus you can tinker with as you see fit, but I wanted to talk to you a bit about your therapeutic responsibilities. Did you work with many adolescents down in New York? No? Then you definitely need to see this to get some idea of what we deal with, with our students. I presume you're aware of the concept of 'the inner child'?"

Reggie nodded. "That's sort of a pop psychology thing, isn't it?"

"Well, a bit. It's an oversimplification of something we've always known about; that the emotional traumas we suffer as children don't go away, even if we think they did. That anger over what was done to us turns inward and manifests itself in any number of ways."

"Mistreated as a child, you mistreat your children," Reggie sad.

"Precisely!" Manx said excitedly. "Yes! Yes! Precisely!"

Reggie gave Frank Cole a quick glance across the conference table and they shared a subtle smile. Manx was in his glory in his expounding, acting as if he was the first to discover this rather basic concept. Cole's look seemed to be flashing, "Humor him!"

"For an example, for an example," Manx bubbled, "Distrust in relationships, suspicion of other people, any number of self-esteem issues --"

"Eating disorders," Reggie offered.

"Oh, yes, yes!" Manx said.

"Insecurity," Frank put in and Reggie realized that the two of them were just throwing things at Manx for their own amusement.

"Definitely, insecurity, high on the list!"

"Substance abuse," Reggie said.

"Yes, yes, we could go on, but the point, I see you get the point, and we use this concept of the inner child, which, I admit, is very, um --"

"Rudimentary?" Frank offered.

"Simplistic?" Reggie threw in.

Manx, thankfully, couldn't tell they were gently poking fun, and ran on: "Yes, yes, simplistic, whatever, the point is it's an easy concept for our student clients to grasp. It's a picture that's clear to them, and that makes working with them to unravel their knots of problems substantially easier. Francis and I have already had some group sessions working with the idea and I want you to watch some of this."

Manx fumbled with the remote control for a bit, managing to turn the TV and the ceiling projector off and on several times and inadvertently skipping ahead on the DVD before getting the video going properly. On the wall screen, Reggie saw what looked like a classroom, desks pushed aside, and seven or eight chairs set up in a circle. The camera was set where she could see Manx and Frank Cole sitting together, although this was obviously Manx's show. Around the circle were a collection of young people -- students, Reggie assumed -- an even mix of girls and boys all around eighteen or nineteen. In the middle of the circle was set a pile of foam blocks with a plastic baseball bat leaning against them.

Manx had, apparently, been talking with a sullen girl in a baggy tie-dyed T-shirt and jeans with hems dragging on the ground.

"And this made you feel how, Alicia?" Manx on the video asked.

Alicia mumbled something into her shirt.

"Come now, Alicia, this is the place where you can say it!" Manx pushed. "Your mother can't hear you in this room. This is your safe space, the place where you can finally say what you feel. It's been in you all this time. Here she is!" Manx stood and made a grand gesture at the pile of foam blocks. "Tell her! Tell her what's been eating at you all these years! Come with me, Alicia," and Manx walked over, took the girl by the hand and led her to the blocks. "Talk to her. Tell her!"

Behind Manx, Reggie could see Frank Cole looking less enthused and eager about where this was going than his superior. She looked across the conference table at live-in-the-flesh Cole and saw him not watching the screen, but eyes downcast with the same concern on his face she saw on the screen.

"Tell her, Alicia," Manx coaxed. "This time, she *has* to hear you. In here, she can't talk you down or ignore you. Tell her."

After a moment, finally, haltingly, in a weak voice, Alicia began: "I know I wasn't in your plan. You keep telling me...how much better things would be...how different if...if I hadn't been born." But now Alicia's voice took on an edge of anger, and she was no longer stumbling over her words. "You treated me like it was *my* fault. You said it so many times you had *me* believing it. But I didn't ask to be born, Mom. If you want to be mad at somebody, shouldn't you be mad at yourself? You made me *hate* myself!"

"You've been punishing yourself, haven't you, Alicia?" Manx said.

"Yes!"

"You've been angry at yourself!"

"Yes!"

Manx picked up the bat and pushed it toward the girl's hands. "But who should you be angry with?"

"Her!"

"Who?"

"My mother!"

"Let it out, Alicia! Let the anger out!"

Alicia brought the bat down on the foam blocks. "I hate you, Mom! *I hate you!*" And the bat came down again, and again, faster, as Alicia started crying hysterically even as she kept wielding the bat.

Then Frank Cole was there, pushing Manx aside, taking Alicia in his arms and stilling the bat in the process. "It's ok, Alicia, it's out, it's done," he cooed, hugging her close, patting her soothingly on the back. "C'mon, let it go, let it go…"

Manx froze the picture there. Reggie must've looked as unsettled as she felt by the emotional explosion on the screen, but that only seemed to amuse Manx. "Did you not deal with this kind of catharsis in your work in New York?"

"Never one displayed so dramatically." She looked over at Frank Cole who was still frowning into his lap.

"Well, Francis here shares the concerns I'm assuming you have. Right, Dr. Cole?"

This seemed to stir Cole from his distracting thoughts. "Hm? Well, Jonathan, I've never said anything --"

"I know, Francis, but you have a face that transmits brighter than any neon sign. I concede that the follow-up to this kind of release is critical. We don't want to just leave these young people shouting their outrage to the heavens. No, of course not. And I'm sure we can refine this approach. Perhaps the three of us can have another dinner discussion at the Clipper at departmental expense." Manx chortled over that. "And if it's too difficult for us to arrange our schedules…" -- and here Manx set his eyes on Reggie -- "…nothing says we can't meet individually for a chat."

"I think all of us together would be best," Reggie said, and took a small amusement at how that seemed to disappoint Manx. "Don't you think so, Dr. Cole?"

Cole was enjoying the moment, too. "One for all and all for one."

Reggie looked back at the screen. Her attention had been on the goings-on in the foreground, but she only now noticed a vaguely familiar face sitting off to the side, almost off the screen. She turned back to Cole. "Isn't that the boy we saw outside?"

Cole nodded. "She means Andy Broder," he explained to Manx.

"Ah, poor young Broder. Did you meet the parents?"

"I saw a little bit of them in action," Reggie said. "Can't say I'm surprised to see him in therapy."

"Yes," Manx said, nodding gravely. "I'm afraid young Broder is still keeping things to himself. But, in time, hopefully…" Manx let it go with a sigh. "Oh, one last thing, Dr. McLaren," Manx said as Reggie and Cole stood to leave, "I know the semester hasn't begun as yet, and informality is the code around here, but I hope once classes begin…" and he made some vague gesture at her rumpled sweats.

"Point taken," Reggie said and headed for the door.

As Reggie and Cole crossed the library lobby, she saw Marcia Danning working behind the front desk. Reggie asked Cole to wait for a second while she went over to the desk. "Hello, Marcia."

Marcia seemed only mildly surprised to see Reggie. "Boy, you're everywhere today."

"When you said you had to get to work, well, I didn't figure it would be here."

"Three days a week here, three days a week at the Burger Barn which is the pit where all these kids like to hang, and classes most nights of the week."

"You're enrolled here?"

"I don't want to be punching due dates and serving taco platters the rest of my life."

Reggie nodded, remembering the textbooks on Marcia Danning's kitchen table: not David's, but his mother's. "That's a lot of time for David to be alone, isn't it? Especially now? I would've thought you'd want some time off because of, you know…"

"And you would've been wrong," Marcia said curtly.

"She's somebody I've been trying to get into therapy," Cole told Reggie as they walked back to their offices. "A lot of open wounds there."

"I didn't know you knew her."

"Not directly." Cole shrugged. "Small town."

"That seems to be everybody's answer to everything around here," Regina said.

"I've been surprised at how much it does explain since I got here."

"What's your opinion of what Manx is doing in those sessions?"

"Actually, I found it a bit frightening. Jonathan seems to think the bigger the detonation the better, but I worry if we're not just letting the genie out of the bottle."

"I'm only glad you were there to bring that poor girl back to earth."

Then they were standing in front of Frank Cole's office door. As he fumbled his keys from his pocket, he said, "Uh, what Jonathan was talking about? About a discussion to re-tune his approach? Maybe we could have a conversation before we meet with him?"

"Now *that* sounds like a line."

Cole smiled embarrassedly. "I didn't mean --"

"But it might not be a bad idea" Reggie said and turned for her office.

She was surprised to find the door partly open. Warily, she gave it a push and found Denny Petit, slouched, and asleep in her desk chair.

"Denny?" she said quietly, touching him lightly on the shoulder.

But it was enough -- cop's reflexes, she thought -- to have him shoot awake so suddenly he almost slid out of the chair. "Oh, God, I'm sorry!" he blurted, still coming fully awake.

"What're you doing here?"

"I'm going over to the Danning house, go through it, see if maybe I could find some -- ...*something*. I thought you might be a help. I came by but you weren't here, I thought I'll just sit for a second..."

"And *phhht*."

"I got the call a little after five this morning and I haven't stopped since."

Reggie plucked at her sweats, wrinkling her nose. "I know the feeling."

"Oh, don't worry, I think --"

"Whatever you do, don't say I look fine just the way I am."

Chapter Four

Even before Reggie pulled to a stop behind Denny Petit's patrol car in front of the Danning house, he was waving at her to stay in her car. He climbed out, pointed to the car in the driveway – a once plush sedan that was yet another piece of typically faded Danning luxury— and then at the house. Reggie saw that someone had torn away the police tape that had crisscrossed the doorway.

But what tipped her curiosity into something more unsettling, that tightened her throat and sent a wave of cold through her, was when she saw Petit walk cautiously up to the front door, his pistol drawn but at his side.

She reached for her cell phone. Should she be calling someone? Who? For what?

She watched Petit try the front door. It was open. Now his pistol was out in front of him as he disappeared inside. Reggie felt her heart pounding so hard her temples throbbed with each beat. She almost collapsed in laughter when she saw Petit reappear in the door, pistol holstered, and a sourly amused look on his face. He beckoned her over, then waved at her to follow him inside and down the hall to the bedroom.

"You'll never guess who's returning to the scene of the crime?" Petit said.

"That's hardly funny," came a voice from the bedroom, then they were in the doorway and there was Alan Danning, going through his dresser drawers and laying clothes in a suitcase lying open on the bed.

"Police work and good taste don't usually go hand in hand, Mr. Danning," Petit said. "You wouldn't be planning a little trip, hm?"

"I've already been on the phone to your office to let them know where they can reach me if they have to."

"And that would be where?"

I'll be staying at the Bayside Motel. It's on the highway just south of town. I'll be there for a while. I...I don't want to stay here. I'm sure you can understand that." He zipped the lid closed on his suitcase. "Now, if you don't mind...?" And he scooped up his suitcase and headed for the door.

Petit didn't move, took the suitcase from him, and tossed it back on the bed. "This is a crime scene, Mr. Danning."

"Which means I can't even take my own clothes?"

"Which means I'd like to look through your bag before you leave."

Disgustedly, Danning unzipped the case and flipped the lid back. "Help yourself." He stepped away from the bed as Petit went through his bag.

"We spoke with your daughter," Reggie said.

"*Step*daughter," Danning corrected harshly.

"Oh, right," Petit said, acid in his voice. "She doesn't seem to care a whole lot for you, Alan. You mind if I call you Alan? Why do you think that is, Alan? Why do you think your stepdaughter doesn't like you much, Alan?"

"I don't know," Danning grumbled. "Typical resentment of a stepparent, I suppose."

"Is that typical, Alan? Dr. McLaren, is that kind of resentment typical?"

"Well," Reggie began, but Petit didn't let her get any further.

"I guess it is, I guess it is," Petit sad. "You see her since she moved out?"

"On the street of course. This is a small town."

"It is that."

"We haven't talked if that's what you mean."

Reggie remembered the photos on the living room mantlepiece. "What about David? Her son? Talk to him?"

"I wouldn't go behind her back like that."

"Because you're a respectful stepparent, right, Alan?" Petit said.

Reggie flashed Petit an irritated look; the bite in his voice wasn't going to help them get useful information. "How about your wife? Did she --"

"I haven't known what she did with her own time for years," Danning said, looking down at the worn bedroom wall-to-wall carpeting. "I haven't wanted to know."

"Like if she saw other men," Reggie suggested.

"Like if she saw other men."

"But as far as you know --"

"I'm saying I don't know." He stepped forward, reached around Petit who was done going through his suitcase for his bag. "Now, if you'll --"

Petit moved so suddenly -- like a detonation -- it was as frightening and startling to Reggie as it obviously was to the wide-eyed Danning as Petit grabbed him by his jacket lapels, spun him and slammed his back against the bedroom wall so hard Reggie could hear the air go out of the man with a *huff.*

"I don't know if you've got blood on your hands or not, Alan," Petit seethed into Danning's face, "but if I hear you've been near Marcia Danning or her son, I swear to Christ --"

Reggie had her hands on Denny's wide shoulders, felt the muscles steel-tight with tension as she tried to pull him back. "Denny! *Denny!*"

Petit let go of Danning with a dismissive brush off, as if letting go of something vile.

"I don't know what you think you know, Petit," Danning gasped.

"Oh, yes you do!"

Danning grabbed his suitcase in his arms and stumbled for the doorway. "You lay your hands on me again, you'll be talking to my lawyer!" and he disappeared out the door.

Petit followed him out, calling out to him the whole way: "If I have occasion to lay my hands on you again, you won't be in any shape to talk to your lawyer or anybody else! Oh, and Alan? Stay around town."

Then Danning was gone and Petit sagged in the front doorway, whatever rage was in him burned off for the moment. Reggie had followed close behind, ready to grab at Petit again if he'd gone for the other man, but now he'd gone from frightening to slope-shouldered and pitiful in just a few seconds. He held up his hands, studied them: they were shaking. He smiled at that, shook his head as if reprimanding himself, then looked up and seemed to notice Reggie for the first time. He lowered his hands, tucked them behind himself.

Reggie offered up what she hoped was a comforting smile. "How about a chat?"

Denny Petit laughed.

He had asked her to follow him, and they had driven to the cove, climbed out of their cars and Reggie tailed after him as he walked to the same jumble of rocks where she and Frank Cole had found him the night before.

He parked himself on the same rock, started patting his pockets, looking for something, then shook his head, remembering. "I threw them away after Frank caught me last night. You wouldn't happen to…?"

Reggie shook her head.

"If you did," he said, smiling slyly, "would you have given me one? What do they call that? Enabling?"

It was her turn to smile. "I don't know," and she took a seat on a rock next to him. The two watched the waters quietly roll in for a bit. "You like this spot."

"Maybe my favorite in the whole town."

Reggie took in the one-hundred-and-eighty-degree view, from Ann Bonano's house to the northern end of the cove where pines almost ran down to the water's edge, the unbroken sea horizon, then the wharf along the southern shore where a handful of lobster boats along with a few recreational powered and sail boats were moored. "I get it," she said quietly.

And after another bit, from Petit: "I'm sorry."

"Don't apologize to me, I wasn't the one you tried to put through a wall." She weighed whether or not to say what was on her mind, then, "I know why you left Chicago. Frank Cole told me. I hope you're not angry with him. He thought, well…"

Petit waved it away; it was ok. "When I started on the force, the old hair bags used to tell me I was too nice, too soft, the streets would eat me up. I remember reading where some shrink said the typical police officer sees more human tragedy in his first three years than most people see in a lifetime. I put nine years in. By that guy's math, that means enough human misery for three lifetimes. I don't have your psychiatric training, but my guess is it took a toll."

"That's a fair guess."

He slid off his rock perch, walked to the water line, stared into the low, gentle surf as if he were looking for something. "Does it get better?"

"It can."

He started patting his pockets, again, an automatic move, then remembered they were empty. "Hell, I can't even quit smoking."

"Well, *that's* hard."

Petit laughed and she joined him.

Then, "Somebody in that family is lying," Reggie said.

"About anything in particular?"

"The picture on the mantle. Marcia said she hadn't seen her mother since she moved out sixteen years ago. Alan Danning says he hasn't been in contact with Marcia or her son in all that time, either. But there's a picture from her wedding there, and another picture of her with David."

"So, which one of them is lying?"

She shook her head. "It doesn't make sense that it's either of them. Why tell a lie so easily proved as a lie?"

Then Petit went stiff. "We have to go back to the house."

Petit stood over the taped outline of Karen Danning's body playing back the recording he'd made when he'd first been examining the crime scene.

Reggie stood back where she couldn't see the rust-colored stain on the rug, like some massive amoeba.

"Something's missing," Petit said, listening to the recording. Something caught his ear. He rewound the recording, started to play it again, signaling to Reggie to listen: *"Hm. Still has her earrings, wedding ring, decent-looking rock, too. Purse on the sofa…"* And Petit pointed to the sofa. No purse.

"He didn't have it with him," Reggie said. "You went through his bags."

"If you were a husband who found himself always cleaning up after your wife, where would you put it? Where do you put your pocketbooks?"

"You mean when they're just not laying around?"

"Slob."

Reggie headed for the bedroom, Petit right behind her. In the bedroom, she went for the one closet and found a half-dozen pocketbooks and purses in a pile on a shelf above the hanging clothes. "I didn't get a good look at it. Do you recognize it?"

Apparently, he did, taking down a slim brown one. He emptied its contents out on the bed, started poking through the litter.

Reggie recognized the usual items: wallet, compact, breath spray, a couple of lipsticks, tissues.

Petit started going through the wallet, then his eyebrows went up as he pulled out a business card. "What do you make of this?"

The card read:

FRANCIS COLE, M.D.

Dept. of Psychology

Diamond Cove University

Faculty/therapy consultations

"You know something about this?" Petit asked.

"If I did, I couldn't say anything."

"Confidentiality."

"Yes."

"You just told me something."

"You've seen how the Dannings were. Any couple with those kinds of problems might look for help."

"That was diplomatically done."

"Thank you." But she could see that Petit could tell she hadn't tipped all her cards, and this time she couldn't find a diplomatic way to tiptoe her way through the dilemma. On the one side were professional ethics, and, to back those up, the law. On the other, there was a brutal

-- hideously brutal -- murder. And Denny Petit. He'd come to Diamond Cove to heal some wounds, Reggie sensed, and she didn't want to do anything to reopen them let alone give him new ones.

He saw it all on her face. "There's something else, isn't there? But you can't talk about it."

She said nothing, made no indication of a response.

Petit sighed but nodded, understanding.

They went back into the living room. Petit peered into the photographs Reggie had told him about, trying to pull something out of them, some clue, some help. "Why would Marcia Danning lie about seeing her mother? It was her *mother*, for Chrissakes. I mean, even if she hated the woman..."

I don't think she did lie, Reggie thought, but I know who would.

Outside, he walked Reggie to her car, held the door open for her. "Listen," he said.

She waited. One minute a raging monster, the next pitiful and wounded, and now... She couldn't help but grin. Now, the bashful boy. "I'm listening."

"Listen," he said, as if starting over might give him the momentum to go on, "Tomorrow I have to take a run down to Portland. The staties have a crime lab down there and I have to bring evidence in: Captain Camo's DNA swab, blood samples, those bed sheets... Well, I was wondering... Have you seen Portland, yet? There is some civilization in Maine. It's not all woods and moose."

"Are you asking me out on a date, Denny?" Oh my God, Reggie thought, he's blushing, again!

"I don't know ferrying crime scene evidence would constitute a date," he said, looking everywhere but at Reggie, "I just thought you might like a drive. I, um…I wouldn't mind the company. We could talk about the case --"

"Oh, God, no!" she laughed. "I think we could both use a break from that."

"Pick you up tomorrow? Around ten?"

She nodded. As she watched him drive off, she remembered what Frank Cole had said to her as he'd walked her home after dinner at the Clipper: *We could all use a friend.*

But whatever warm thoughts went with that idea quickly evaporated as Reggie climbed out of her car after Denny Petit's had driven out of sight and headed back toward the Danning house.

Reggie found David Danning plopped on the floor of his building's front porch, slumped against the railing, his eyes locked on his cell phone, his busy thumbs suggesting he was focused on a videogame.

"Locked out?" Reggie asked.

The boy didn't look up. "Got a key," he mumbled. "Just felt like some air."

Reggie parked against the railing next to him where she could look over his shoulder. "Some air…with a game."

Same mumble: "I's bored."

"It's a shame about your grandmother. I'm sorry."

He shrugged.

"How's your mom taking it?"

Another shrug. "Weird."

"Not like you think she should."

A bare nod. "Mm. Yeah. Weird."

"She made your grandmother off limits to you, didn't she?"

A brief pause for his flying thumbs. "Lotta things she doesn't want me to do," and he went back to his game.

Reggie gave what she hoped sounded like a sympathetic sigh. "Doesn't seem fair, her dragging you into whatever issues she had with your grandmother. But she's your mom, and you always do what she says, right?"

Another brief pause. "Doesn't matter. She's always on my case 'bout somethin'."

"I'll bet she'd *really* be on you if she knew you'd given these to your grandmother," and Reggie held the two photographs she'd removed from their frames at Karen Danning's house -- the wedding photo and the picture of Marcia and David -- in front of the boy's eyes.

David pushed the pictures aside, scrambled to his feet and headed for the front door.

Before Reggie could call to him, Marcia Danning's voice from the front walk: "What the hell's goin' on here?"

Which was enough of a distraction to Reggie for David to disappear inside.

Marcia Danning lumbered up onto the porch, laden with a tote bag stuffed with textbooks and notepads, and a bag of groceries in the other. "You can't question my son without me, and now that I'm here, fuck off."

"I'm not a police officer, Marcia. I just wanted to know about these." Reggie held up the photos.

Marcia's eyes went wide. She set down her bags and grabbed the photos from Reggie's hand. For a moment, Marcia's face softened, a finger gently touched the figures in the photos. Reggie was glad the blood spatter had been kept from the photos by the glass in the frame. Then Marcia's face went cold. "Where'd you get these?"

"Your mother's house."

"My mother's --? How the hell did she --?"

"Well, that's the question, Marcia, isn't it?"

Marcia shoved the photos back at Reggie and reached for her bags.

"You want to talk about your stepfather?" Reggie asked.

"I was told anything I said was confidential."

"Told by who?"

It was clear, then, that Marcia had said something she suddenly realized she shouldn't have said. "Get outta here."

"Does David know?"

Marcia Danning's face went to a different kind of cold; a rage burning like ice. "I see you around my son, again, or you talk to me about anything more than late fees on a borrowed book, I'm not gonna talk to a lawyer, I'm not gonna talk to that cop you were here with -- I'm just gonna lay you out, lady. Understand?"

The front door slammed closed behind her.

Back in New York, Reggie jogged on a treadmill. Sidewalks were too crowded, she didn't trust the parks at night, but Diamond Cove in the evening threatened neither. And the scenery -- the open fields bordered by dense stands of timber on the inland side, the cove taking on the setting sun's amber glow on the ocean side, the sky flashed with gold turning to a brilliant crimson above -- was infinitely better.

As she turned back toward Ann Bonano's house, she bounced through the intersection that was downtown, the only lit windows among the shops those of the Clipper. She would have trotted right on past except she caught a glimpse of Frank Cole sitting by himself at the bar. She considered her garb -- the same sweats she'd been wearing all day -- then remembered the head-to-toe camouflage ensemble of the improbably named Peter O'Toole, feeling if the Clipper could accept *that* as acceptable evening wear… She went in.

"Evening, Frank."

He'd been deep in thought, staring down into his drink, hadn't noticed her even as she slid onto the stool next to him.

"Reggie!" Surprise went to a smile, he offered to buy her a drink, but she asked only for a tall glass of ice water. "Understandable," Cole said and called the bartender over. "Do you have a whole ensemble of these?" and he gestured at her sweats, "or is this the same outfit --"

"Long day, Frank, have a little mercy. Just be glad I'm upwind of you."

"One man's reek is another man's perfume," and they both chuckled.

"All things considered, Frank, don't you think you should've told me you were treating Karen Danning?"

which effectively killed Cole's chuckle. "You know Denny has me helping him with this. You pushed him at me, for God's sake."

Cole nodded at Reggie to follow him to an empty booth. They sat across from each other.

"Because I couldn't tell him," Cole said. "You know that. I thought you would be able to put it together for him."

"And you couldn't tell him you were treating her daughter, either." Before he could ask Reggie how she knew, "I was just talking to her. She let it slip. I think I can pretty much put it together." She looked to make sure no one was close by, tilted her head close to Cole, her voice almost a whisper: "Alan Danning molested his stepdaughter. Typical in these cases, Karen Danning either deluded herself into believing he wasn't, or she knew but, for one reason or another, did nothing. Which explains why, years later, they all hate each other and why half the family is in therapy. Did mom and/or daughter know the other one was seeing you?"

"No."

"Why the hell didn't Karen Danning at least throw Alan's ass out?"

"You'd never know it to look at them, but at one time she was in love with him. Or she's convinced herself she was. I think she was just tired of being lonely. She didn't want to go back to that."

"Marcia left sixteen years ago. Why in God's name were Alan and Karen still together?"

"I think he wouldn't divorce because he was afraid of what'd come out."

"And her?"

"Staying with him was how she was punishing him. And, I think, maybe punishing herself."

Reggie shook her head. "Jesus, what they don't teach you in Psych 101. Does the son, Marcia's kid, David, what does he know?"

"According to Marcia, nothing."

"He might know more than Marcia thinks. I think David was seeing grandma on the sly." Reggie told him about the photographs.

Cole nodded. "Makes sense. Mom says you can't see your grandmother, he wants to know why, she won't tell, he gets curious, in a town this small they're going to bump into each other, grandma feels guilty and tries to atone by being nice to the grandson. Throw in some natural teen you're-not-the-boss-of-me…"

Reggie sat back in the booth, sagged against the back of the seat with a sigh. "It feels like a fucking soap opera."

Cole smiled. "New England has been producing great soap operas since *The Scarlet Letter*. Look, you have the day off tomorrow, enjoy your ride and put it out of your mind."

He obviously enjoyed her surprise. "How did you know…?"

Cole's smile turned mischievous. "The ever-chivalrous Denny Petit checked in with me, wanting to make sure he wasn't, um, I think the word he used was 'encroaching.' I was impressed with his vocabulary."

Remembering how Cole and Jonathan Manx had been competing for her attention, it was Reggie's turn for a sly smile. "So… *Is* he 'encroaching'?"

Cole shifted uncomfortably in his seat. "Well, it's not like the thought hasn't crossed my mind a time or six, and I still wouldn't mind a dinner to discuss departmental matters if for no other reason than to one-up Jonathan Manx…but for now, I defer to my friend."

"He's not the only one who's chivalrous. 'For now'?"

"Well, I'm no saint, and if my dear friend bobbles the ball…"

Reggie finished her water and stood. She could see Cole was wondering if perhaps he'd overstepped. She gave him an 'it's-ok' nod. "I wouldn't mind messing with Jonathan, either. How about we talk about a dinner next week?"

Cole held up his drink. "Here's to the Temporary Friend DMZ!"

She left laughing.

The sun had almost slipped behind the horizon sending brilliant rays of red and gold across the sky as she turned from the beach toward Ann Bonano's house. As if she hadn't moved since the night before, she saw Ann, again, on her beach recliner, drink in hand.

"Don't you ever do anything but lay around and sip cocktails?"

"Do you ever wear any real clothes? C'mon up, sweets, I've got your glass chilling."

Reggie climbed the narrow stairs, threaded through the usual jumble in Ann's studio and was soon sliding into the recliner alongside. Instead of martini glasses, Ann was serving in coupes.

"What're we drinking tonight?"

"Another old folks' drink: Manhattans."

They sat enjoying the sunset for a moment, watching the sky slowly dull to a darkening blue.

Then, from Ann: "You packing a picnic lunch tomorrow, or you two gonna eat in Portland? I can make recommendations."

Reggie almost fell out of her chair. "How the hell --. Oh, right, small town. People in this place all have some kind of radar?"

Ann laughed, drained her drink, and poured a fresh one from the shaker on the floor by her chair. "I'm not a native Mainer. Moved here with my husband from Providence, he got a job teaching Poli Sci at the school, and I rode in on his coattails. When we first got here, I was told the good thing about up here is nobody really gives a good goddamn what you do; everybody minds their own business. The bad news is everybody knows everybody else's business…and they talk about it. 'S he a nice fella?"

"Mostly."

"Ah," she said warily.

"He's got demons, Ann."

Ann lay her head against the seat back, looked up at the darkening sky with a sigh. "We all have demons, sweetheart. The trick is keeping them on a leash."

"How do you know if someone can do that?"

Ann gave up a low, rueful chuckle. "Sad to say you don't find out 'til you get bit."

Chapter Five

Denny Petit showed up in front of Ann Bonano's house in a husky SUV caked in dried mud. Whatever he does in his off hours, Reggie thought, being in his SUV must be like riding a rodeo bronc when he does it.

He stepped out to open her door for her. There was something nicely softer about him out of uniform in his jeans and plaid shirt. She matched him in her own jeans and a white pullover. Hearing how easily Maine could get chilly even in late August, she had brought a denim jacket with her (Ann Bonano had referred to it as a "Canadian tuxedo").

"So, this is what you look like in *real* clothes," Denny grinned as he helped her up into the SUV.

"I like to spruce up for a visit to a crime lab." She looked around the vehicle. "Where are the samples? In the back? Are they going to be safe back there?"

Denny shuffled on his feet and looked at the ground. "I, um, have a confession," he mumbled. "State crime lab isn't in Portland. 'S in Augusta."

"Augusta."

"But Augusta's a long ride and, frankly, there's not much there to, well…"

"Well, what?" she said, enjoying the shuffling and, good God, there was that blush of his, again.

Denny finally straightened up and looked her in the eye. "Thing is I need to get out of town for a while. This has all been too much…"

"I get it. Well, that part of it. But what am *I* doing here?"

She enjoyed prodding him, she knew Denny could see it and it looked like he was starting to enjoy being prodded. "I didn't want to go by myself, ok? Look, Reggie, I wouldn't blame you if you, um…"

She pulled the door closed, shot an arm and pointing finger forward: "Excelsior!"

Denny smiled. "I don't know what that means, but I'll take it as a positive."

Coming in from the north, Rt. 295 took them close to the north shore of Casco Bay. The seaward side of the city extended out into the bay on a blunt peninsula, looking on maps something like a swollen thumb. The peninsula ground sloped upward toward the sea, its heights crowded with old Victorian era buildings most of which had been carved up into apartments, and newer constructions: condos made pricey by virtue of their ocean view. Running inland, Reggie was impressed to see Portland actually had a skyline; hardly the eye-filling, spire-filled panorama of a Manhattan, but more than she had expected.

Petit drove them up the heights into a leisurely busy downtown of banks and office buildings. "I will never understand," Petit said, "how there could be so little money in this state, and so many damn banks!"

He found a parking garage and then walked them down toward the waterfront on the south side of town, the part of the city Petit said was called The Old Port, a maze of narrow cobblestoned streets and buildings of old red brick or clapboard.

"I'm told at one time it was getting pretty dumpy down here," Petit said. "But they took a cue from what Boston did with that area around Faneuil Hall. They gutted the buildings, left the shells to keep that old-timey look, and then bit by bit, it came back. All these little shops, coffee places, new restaurants, down by the waterfront clubs started opening up."

They walked the cobbles of the Old Port, stopping at shop windows offering a surprisingly (to Reggie) rich array, from stylish clothes to kitschy Maine souvenirs.

Denny held up a finger outside of one shop, its window nearly blotted out by touristy T-shirts: sunbathing lobsters, and sunglassed moose kicking back in lounge chairs sucking on a can of Molson. "I noticed your office was kind of empty," he said.

"Kind of?"

"I've got a cell back at the station that's got a warmer feel to it. Stay here." Five minutes later, he was back on the sidewalk with a paper bag.

Reggie looked inside at a jumble of plushy bodies. "What's this?"

"To keep you company in your office. A puffin. And a moose. You're in Maine, you should at least have a moose."

Reggie laughed. "Thank you. That's very… It's very sweet, Denny."

They stood looking at each other awkwardly for a moment, Reggie nervously fingering the bag. She was grateful when Denny broke the quiet:

"You hungry? There's some nice places here, as good as anything we had back in Chicago, but for your first trip, I want to get you something authentic."

They walked down to the waterfront, which was a mix of docks for sight-seeing boats, some pretty impressive sailboats and powered yachts.

"I thought you said nobody here had money," Reggie said, pointing to a cabin cruiser nearly as big as Ann Bonano's house.

"*Most* don't. But the few that do, have a *lot*. But a lot of these don't belong to Mainers. Quite a few -- maybe most -- belong to out-of-staters who vacation here, money people from Massachusetts, New York. Fifty weeks a year, these things just sit here."

"What kind of money do you have to have to keep one of these things tied up for fifty weeks a year?"

"More than you and I will ever see," and they shared an agreeing nod and laugh.

A bit further along the waterfront, away from the bustle of the heart of the Old Port was a wharf area looking like it hadn't changed in decades: clapboard buildings sagging with age and beaten gray with weather, and moored along the docks, working lobster boats. Denny parked Reggie outside a small eatery which looked like something out of an Edward Hopper painting. He soon came out with two paper bags and a, "Follow me."

They walked for fifteen minutes or so, following the waterfront up into the peninsula heights. As they neared the crest, the city retreated to one side of the boulevard that ran along the crest, and on the other side was parkland running down to the bay. Denny found them a bench alongside a walking path that wound down toward the water. Below them was nearly the whole of Casco Bay, from where the shoreline ran to Falmouth on the north, to the southern part of the bay where Portland Head Light stood sentinel, its white-washed tower as bright a beacon as its light in the sun of a clear, bracingly breezy day.

"I didn't know what you drank, and I was afraid coffee would get cold, so I got you a soda," Denny said, setting the bags between them and pulling out a pair of take-out cups. "I hope that's ok. Now for a bit of *real* Maine."

"More than a puffin and a moose?"

"Well, it kind of fills out the picture."

Denny reached into the other bag and unwrapped what she thought was tuna in a hot dog roll. Before she could ask, he held up a finger to silence her and held it out.

She took a whiff, thought she recognized the aroma, enough so to take an eager bite. "Oh, God, that's good!"

"Lobster roll. I've never had a bad one, but some places make better ones, and that little dive makes the best. I got us two apiece."

"Good call," she managed through a mouthful. "Although I'm thinking about how many laps I'm going to have to run around Diamond Cove to burn this off."

"Just enjoy."

They sat quietly, eating, only this time the silence didn't feel awkward.

Denny started on his second lobster roll, took a deep lungful of the salty breeze coming off the bay. "Ya know, I could sit here forever."

Reggie couldn't remember ever seeing Denny's face so at peace. It had always seemed deep in thought, concentrating, a furrow permanently dug between his thick brows. She almost hated to say what was on her mind…but not enough to hold it back. "Can I ask you something?"

"Since I practically shanghaied you into coming, I guess I owe you."

"I hate to ruin the mood, but I have to ask…"

He shrugged; go ahead, but she still felt a certain amount of guilt as she saw his eyebrows knit, the furrow taking up residence between them again.

"Why are you still a cop? Frank told me why you left Chicago. Don't be mad at him."

Denny shook his head; it didn't matter. A rueful smile: "Thing is I don't know how to do anything else. I am trapped by my resume. If I could figure out something else to do, I'd quit tomorrow."

"Why did you become a policeman in the first place?"

"It never occurred to me to do anything else," he sighed. "My father was with the department. His two brothers. My grandfather. Growing up, I thought, well, it just always seemed to me this is what the Petits do. Funny thing is the warning flags were always there. My father made it to retirement, then died of a heart attack just two years later. He was only sixty-six. My one uncle drank himself to death, the other was pushed out the second time they busted him for beating his wife."

"And your grandfather?"

Denny gave up a wryly amused smile. "Maybe it was different in his day. He died when I was still a kid, but he was that old-fashioned beat cop you see in the old movies; took care of the people on his beat, always carried candy for the kids, but if you got out of line, he didn't have a problem cracking you on the head with his billy. In his day, the department didn't have a problem with it, either."

Reggie was even more reluctant to ask the next question. Denny must've seen it in her face and nodded at her to go ahead. "Were you ever married?"

He nodded. "You know what the divorce rate is for city police officers?"

"Somewhere between appalling and horrific."

He laughed. "The station house newsletters were filled with ads for divorce lawyers. I don't blame her. We split when…when what happened, happened."

"Why did you go off on that guy?"

Another sigh. "You don't have to be Sigmund Freud to figure it out. He was treating his wife the way my dad treated my mom."

And before she knew it, her hand was settling on his forearm. "I'm enjoying today, Denny. I'm glad you shanghaied me."

He looked out at the bay. "I'm sorry you saw --. Well, the way I got with that Danning guy."

"I won't say it wasn't a little scary."

"A little?"

"I crapped a little in my pants. But just a little."

"You're generous," he laughed.

"Someone said something to me recently, something people in my field learn early on: everybody has demons."

"What's yours? Oh crap." His cell phone was buzzing. "Text from Grace. Oh-oh." His face clouded.

"What?"

"We have to get back," and he started scooping up napkins and sandwich wrappings, shoving them into one of the empty bags. "Now. This lets all the Dannings off the hook."

"What happened?"

"There's been another murder."

"Oh my God…"

"My thought exactly."

She watched as he paused for a moment, stopping to take one last look out at the rich blue waters of the bay, then his chest heaved, he shook his head, and let out a short, sighed, "Shit…"

Chapter Six

The Bayside Motel was a typically nondescript roadside motel, sitting along the county highway leading into Diamond Cove from the south. It was noteworthy in only two respects:

It's rank of rooms was surprisingly long for an area offering very little in the way of commerce or recreation, but it had been explained to Reggie when she'd mentioned this during her interview visit that the often-surplus capacity was for the surges in parents that came with the beginning and end of every semester at the university.

And, despite its name, it was nowhere even close to being in view of the shoreline. This, too, had been explained to Reggie with what she had come to consider to be typical Maine prosaic thinking: nobody would know that when they called for reservations.

Even before Denny Petit's SUV came around a bend in the forest-lined road, Reggie could see blue and red flashing lights -- police and ambulance -- splashing along the trees across from the Bayside. Denny pulled to a corner of the lot far from the crowd growing around an open door to one of the rooms.

"Fucking people," Denny sighed as he watched a pickup and then another car whip into the parking lot only to disgorge their riders to join the crowd of gawkers.

Reggie recognized the two police officers keeping the crowd away from the door as the same two she'd seen at the Danning house. Denny tooted his horn and waved one of them over; Mondry, the policeman Reggie remembered as being sick in Karen Danning's backyard. He looked just as shaken and sick to his stomach now as he had then.

"Who is it?" Denny asked him.

Mondry leaned against the car door and for a moment, Reggie thought he might vomit in the window. The young policeman took a deep breath. "Husband and wife --"

"Oh, Christ," Denny said, sagging in his seat. *Both* of them?"

Mondry gulped, again looking like he was trying to quiet his stomach as he nodded. "Registered yesterday as Charles and Eloise Broder. They checked in yesterday --"

But Reggie wasn't hearing Mondry's rundown. All she could hear in her head was "Broder...*Broder.*"

She began to refocus as Mondry was saying, "Just like that Danning lady. Maid found them when she came to change the sheets. That would've been about an hour and a half ago. We called you soon's we got the report."

"Weapon?" Denny asked.

"Like I said: just like the Danning business. Ball peen hammer. Found it in the bathroom sink. Haven't touched anything, Chief, I remembered that business you said, integrity of the crime scene 'n' all."

"Good job, Mooney --"

"Mondry," Reggie corrected.

Denny looked to the patrolman who nodded in agreement. "Go back and help what's-his-face and no, I don't care what his name is, just go help him make sure none of these buzzards go clomping around the crime scene. Don't even let the ambulance guys in until I have a chance to work the scene."

Mondry nodded and ran back toward the room.

"You knew them?" Denny asked.

That was the first time Reggie was aware something must've been showing on her face. "I think so. If it's who I think they are, their kid goes to --. Oh, Christ!"

"What's the matter, Reggie?"

She was already climbing out of the car, pulling her cell phone out of her jacket pocket. "Do you need me here?"

"I can talk you through it later. What's going --"

She was already punching Frank Cole's number into her phone. Cole's phone began to ring. "C'mon, answer, answer! Jesus, Frank, please --!"

"Reggie?"

Oh, God, had she been saying all that out loud?

She was surprised at how distant Denny sounded. She looked around and saw she had already started walking toward the highway in the direction of Diamond Cove. Denny was still back at his SUV.

"Reggie!"

"I'll call you later!" she yelled back to Denny, then almost gasped in relief when Frank Cole picked up. "It's Reggie."

"Reggie? I thought you were --"

"That Broder kid," she said breathlessly, "the one we saw the other day when you were showing me around, the kid with the shitty parents --"

"Yeah, Andy."

"Do you know their names?"

"Who, the parents? Sure. I've talked to Andy enough about them. Charles -- well, everybody calls him Chuck -- and --"

"Eloise?"

"Yeah," and now Cole sounded alarmed. "How do you know?"

"Goddamn, I wish I didn't. I'm at the Bayside Motel. They found his parents murdered there a little while ago.".

"Oh my --"

"Just like Karen Danning. If that boy --"

"He's in one of the dorms. I'm home. It's going to take me about 10 minutes to get there. Where are you?"

"I'm walking in from the Bayside. Can you swing by and pick me up on the county road?"

Cole rang off.

"Changes things, doesn't it?" Reggie turned. It was Alan Danning, standing in the Bayside parking lot, nodding at the crowd around the Broders' open door where Denny was just passing through, camera and voice recorder in hand. Reggie remembered: this was where Danning had said he'd be staying. "No way you people can try to pin *this* one on me."

Reggie stopped, turned, walked back to Alan Danning, stood in front of him, looking him in his small, gloating eyes. He was waiting for a response, a rebuttal, but damned if Reggie could find something appropriate.

For the first time in her life, Reggie McLaren was glad her father had wanted a son instead of a daughter. He had tried to compensate as dads who wind up with daughters instead of sons do: taking her out to the park with a bat and ball to shag flies, tossing a football back and forth in their yard, and when her mother carped about her dad tomboying her up, her father came back with, "Here's one a girl living in that psycho city could use!" to justify showing her how to throw a punch.

Which, after coming up dry with a response to Alan Danning and muttering, "Oh, fuck it," she did, landing it squarely on the side of Danning's jaw, dropping him painfully on his ass on the punishingly hard pavement.

It was, she reprimanded herself -- if mildly -- an unforgivable professional lapse. But as she looked down at Danning, rubbing his bruised jaw, staring up at her incredulously, she just shrugged, and finally dredged up something appropriate to say. "Sometimes, Mr. Danning, there are no words," and then turned and went on her way.

Even before the dorms came into view, Reggie knew they were too late by the students she saw running in from all points on the small campus toward the quad.

"Oh no," Cole sighed as he turned his car into the drive leading to the quad parking lot and saw two campus security cars, their blue roof lights flashing, pulled up on the lawn in front of one of the dorms, security men trying to clear students from the wide portico. The dorm's fire alarm was clanging away, and joining the din was the rise-and-fall wail of an ambulance siren closing in.

Cole parked in the dorm lot, then sat for a moment, staring at his white-knuckled fists clenched around the steering wheel. After a moment, his fists relaxed, he sighed heavily, killed the engine, and reached for the door.

"Do you want me to go with you?" Reggie asked.

Cole shook his head, climbed slowly out of the car, and headed for the dorm. Reggie saw him pull one of the security men aside, there was a brief exchange as they shouted to each other over the clanging alarm, then Cole trudged heavily up the stairs of the dorm, crossed the portico, and disappeared inside.

He reappeared a few minutes later, looking somehow shrunken, sag-shouldered, barely noticing the ambulance crew, now arrived, as they pushed past him with a stretcher.

When he climbed back into his car, Reggie saw his eyes were wet and red. "I don't know what those EMTs are hurrying for," he said.

The fire alarm cut off. The silence in the car that followed was a relief…but solemn.

"Good," Frank said. "Thing was giving me a headache. The security guys pulled the alarm to clear the building."

"Andy?" Reggie's throat was so tight the sound came out broken and raspy.

"I'd read about it," Cole said with an unsettling lifelessness, "but I didn't really think you could do it."

"Frank…"

"Hung himself from his shower head with a belt." He reached inside his jacket for his cell phone. "I better call Denny." But his hands were shaking so badly, he couldn't cleanly punch the numbers.

She put a hand on Cole's, gave it a squeeze while she took his phone with the other. "I'll do it."

"Good," he said and started climbing out of the car again, "because I'm going to go somewhere and be sick."

Chapter Seven

They were sitting around the table in the same conference room in the university's library where Jonathan Manx had shown Reggie the video of one of his "inner child" sessions. Manx sat at the head of the table, his usually ebullient face now stony and locked on the smooth, featureless polished wood of the table. Reggie sat close to Frank Cole on one side of the table, Denny Petit across from her. Outside the room's high-set windows, the sky was shot with a late-day blood red.

Denny broke off his exchange with Cole when he saw Reggie massaging the bruised knuckles of her right hand. "You ok? Something the matter with your hand?

"Just a cramp."

Denny's tongue poked at the inside of his cheek. "Cramp, huh?"

Reggie flushed. He knows, she thought.

Thankfully, he turned back to Cole. "What were you saying, Frank? You can't tell me anything about this kid?"

Cole sighed. "Confidentiality --"

"What confidentiality, Frank? Jesus, the kid's dead!"

Manx cleared his throat. "The principle still applies," he said quietly, never taking his eyes from the tabletop. "People who need help might stop coming to us if they thought their most personal secrets would be revealed after their deaths."

Denny's face started to go red. "You told *her* about *me!*" he barked at Cole, pointing at Reggie.

Cole squirmed in his seat. "You were never formally in therapy, Denny. I always looked at it as a conversation between friends."

Denny huffed. "I'm trying to decide if you're a shitty therapist or a shittier friend."

"Right now," Cole mumbled, "I'm feeling like both."

"Which is an issue for another day," Manx said curtly, cutting off the digression. "My question is --. Denny, when were the bodies found? You said a maid discovered the bodies…?"

"Around two."

"And by the time you got back to Diamond Cove, the poor boy was already… I'm wondering how he found out so quickly."

"Small towns," Reggie said quietly.

"Yes," said Manx.

"Do you have a time of death on the parents?" Cole asked Denny.

"I'll know better after the autopsy, but by the degree of rigor when I got there, I'd ballpark it sometime early this morning."

"Seven? Eight? Nine?"

"Yeah, something like that. Why?"

Cole only shook his head.

"How about this?" Denny tried. "Can you tell me if this kid was capable of bashing his parents' heads in? Can you tell me that much?"

Cole weighed the question for a second. "Doubtful."

"Doubtful you can tell me, or doubtful he could do it?"

"Doubtful he could do it."

"Doubtful." Denny shook his head in frustration. "That's kind of mushy, Frank."

Reggie was disappointed Denny was taking a typical outsider's view of the practice, assuming that it dealt in definites, in precise causes and effect. Manx may have decided to sulk and let Denny Petit hammer away at Cole, but Reggie couldn't. "Look, Denny, there's hardly a human being on the planet that pushed in the right way under the right circumstances isn't capable of killing. You're an experienced police officer; you *know* that. It doesn't mean they *will*."

"I didn't think he had it in him," Cole said, "Alright?"

"Then why did he kill himself?" Denny pressed.

Cole sighed. "Actually, I can think of a half-dozen reasons. Maybe he knew he'd be suspected. And for someone who didn't make many friends -- and that was the case with Andy -- maybe the loss of his parents --"

"Even lousy parents?"

"Yes, even lousy parents, was too much, he felt too alone. And then there's guilt."

Denny flashed a triumphant so-I-was-right quick smile at Reggie before turning back to Cole. "So, you *do* think he --"

"I don't think Frank means that kind of guilt," Reggie said. Denny gave her a whose-side-are-you-on glare from which Reggie didn't flinch, didn't turn away.

"Have you ever in your life -- casually, not seriously -- wished someone dead?" Cole asked. "'Boy, my life would be so much easier if old So-and-So got hit by a train.' Well, Andy had a lot of reasons to wish that on his parents. But then, what happens when the wish comes true? For someone with Andy's issues... *That* kind of guilt. Andy was a textbook case of victim precipitation --"

Which drew a blank look from Denny.

"Meaning the victim contributes to their own victimization, compounded in Andy's case by him being both the victim and victimizer." Cole shook his head. "Any of those reasons I mentioned, maybe all of them, hammering away at the boy's fault lines. I've had a suspicion he was capable of suicide, but I wasn't -- ..." Cole poked at his forehead with an index finger, hard enough to make Reggie wince. "I should've kept a closer watch on him," saying it like a hard self-reprimand.

"Give yourself a break, Frank," Reggie said. "Who knew something like this was going to happen?"

"You're sure it was suicide?" Cole asked Petit.

"No forced entry, no signs of a struggle."

"What about the parents?" Reggie asked. "Any idea how that played out?"

"Just like Karen Danning. No forced entry. Looks like the dad was hit first, blitzed from behind, then the mom from the front. It must've happened fast; no defensive wounds on her. Then once they were down...

Just like Karen Danning. I'm going over there later to dust for prints. If the maids there do their job, it'll be easy to pick up anything that doesn't belong. But if they're a bit sloppy, well, it's a motel, guests in and out, it'll be a nightmare; prints on prints on prints. Going to check the kid's room, too, but a dorm room… Like a hive, another mess."

Manx finally looked up. "What's your thinking, Denny? When it was Karen Danning, the obvious suspects were her husband, maybe the daughter…"

"I was even wondering about maybe the kid for a while," Denny said, "The daughter's boy. But now… Frank, without violating your goddamned confidentiality, you knew the boy, this Broder, you worked with Karen Danning. Is there any connection between the families? You can tell me that much, right?"

Cole shook his head. "None that I know of. The Broders lived in a small town a hundred miles north of here, always did. The Dannings have always lived here. Kids in different schools. The families didn't even know each other existed as far as I know. But it was obviously the same killer."

"Or someone who wanted it to look like the same killer."

"Who?" Manx asked. "Other than the Broder boy, do you have any other suspects?"

Denny sighed and shook his head.

"Which means…" Whatever it was Manx was thinking was too unpalatable to utter. He shuddered and went back to studying the tabletop.

"I think what Jonathan doesn't want to say," put in Cole, "is we might be looking at a random serial killer." It was as much a question to Denny as a conclusion.

Denny frowned. "I don't even want to think about that possibility."

"But these killings weren't random," Reggie said, and three sets of eyes turned to her.

"How so?" Denny asked.

"Commonalities. There's no forced entry in either case, no struggle. Whoever it was, it was somebody they all trusted enough to let in and let get close."

Denny mulled this a moment, gave a slight agreeing nod. "I'm going to get in touch with the FBI's profilers down in Quantico and see if they maybe can give me something to work with. In fact, I'm going over to the office right now and call them."

But as Denny started to rise, Manx stopped him with, "One more item, Denny. One way or another, all of these victims had connections to our program. Have you been getting any calls from the press?"

"Luckily, they don't have what you might consider a state paper in this state, but I am starting to get some calls from the regional dailies and the TV people. And the mayor's been in my ear; apparently, he's been getting calls, too."

Manx nodded, unsurprised. "I've been in talks with the president of the university, and she feels -- if it doesn't interfere with your investigation, Denny -- that she'd like to keep that aspect -- the connection to our program -- quiet if we could, or at least downplay it. The program is just getting on its feet, and this could be very damaging both to the program, and because of that, to the university. We do have to consider the larger picture here."

"For Christ's sake, Jonathan!" Cole exploded, slapping a hand down on the table, a sound sharp enough to make Reggie jump. "Four people are dead! Is there a bigger picture than that?"

Reggie was impressed that Manx hadn't flinched.

"I appreciate that, Francis. I hope *you* appreciate *my* -- and the *president's* -- position. This has been a great tragedy to the concerned families. Let's not let the tragedy metastasize." At that, Manx slowly rose from his seat and headed for the conference room door. "Keep us apprised, Denny, won't you?"

"Of course."

And the door closed behind him.

The three sat for a moment, Denny flashing harsh glares at both Reggie and Cole before giving a dismissive huff and storming for the door.

"Denny?" Reggie called after him, but he left without a response.

Then it was Reggie and Frank Cole sitting quietly for a moment, before Cole broke the silence: "I appreciate your coming to my defense, but I hate to think I might've created a problem for you two."

Reggie dismissed his concerns with a head shake, but she was thinking the same thing.

"Which reminds me; not that it's any of my business, but how was your --"

"Don't call it a date, Frank," Reggie said with a wince. "And is this the time for that kind of conversation?"

He nodded.

"Are you going to be alright?" she asked. "I mean, the boy, Andy Broder; you couldn't know, Frank. Sometimes --"

He was already nodding, knowing what she was going to say, but they both knew how hollow anything she could say was going to sound.

"Can I buy you a drink?" she asked.

He smiled a thanks. "I'd like to be by myself for a bit. Think I'll go for a long walk."

"I understand. Well, then..."

They both stood, Cole held the door open for her.

"One last thing," he said, "About Denny. I just want to, again, repeat a caution."

"You already told me about his past, and we had a nice, productive conversation about that. Which is what I always thought you wanted."

"It was. What time did Denny pick you up this morning?"

"About ten. Why?"

"And Denny said the Broders were killed maybe an hour or more before that."

"And...?"

"Commonalities."

"What?"

"You said it had to be somebody both Karen Danning and the Broders trusted enough to let in and get close."

"Ok."

"Only two possibilities come to mind. One is someone they both knew, and since there's no connection between the families, I can't think of who that could possibly be."

"And possibility Number Two?"

"Who doesn't trust a policeman knocking at their door?"

Outside, the sky had gone from red to black.

Reggie sat in her car at the foot of the drive -- a wide, muddy path, really -- that led up to the trailer home where Denny Petit lived. The trailer was set back from the road, well into the dense woods around Diamond Cove, and Reggie -- Frank Cole's cautions still echoing in her head -- didn't like the fact that she couldn't see the lights of another residence in any direction. Even the trees disappeared into the inky night. To someone who had lived all her life in and around big cities, just the idea that there were stretches of road and town without streetlights -- or lights of any kind -- was unnerving.

She kept telling herself as she sat in her idling car that this was a bad idea, in part because of the possibility Frank Cole had raised, but for Reggie, in larger part, because this was a step toward opening a door, she wasn't sure she wanted to open. But what weighed against all that was how she had felt sitting next to Denny earlier in the day -- Good God, had that just been that afternoon? -- looking out over Casco Bay, and how just sitting quietly together had seemed so...natural. It was an occasion and a feeling she had denied herself all her adult life.

She didn't know how long she sat there, debating whether to roll up that drive or turn around and go home, but then she saw a silhouette in one of the trailer's windows. Denny must've seen the glow of her headlights and grown curious as to why they hadn't passed by or moved up the drive.

Ok, Chickenshit, Reggie said to herself, moved her foot from the brake to the gas pedal and sent her car slipping and sliding up the muddy inclined drive.

By the time she had pulled up alongside Denny's SUV, her messy ride up the drive had made enough noise to bring Denny to his doorway, his broad-shouldered form a dark silhouette against the low lights from inside.

She killed the engine but didn't get out right away, then told herself, Well, you came this far, schmuck, and climbed out.

She could see Denny leaning forward, peering into the dark, finally stepping aside to let some of the room light behind him spill out into the night, splashing across Reggie.

"Reggie?"

"I hope I'm not disturbing anything."

Denny's shoulders shook slightly with a small chuckle. "It's Diamond Cove, Reg. There's never a social life to interrupt."

"Can I come in?"

"Sure."

He stepped aside as she climbed up some "stairs" of piled cinderblocks.

"I think I've got mud on my shoes," she said, trying to kick the clumps loose against the top step.

"Don't worry about it."

She stepped into a cramped living room: a small sofa, two easy chairs, a big screen TV tuned to one of the documentary channels. Next to one of the easy chairs on a folding TV table, an open pizza box, a few slices gone, a water glass partly filled with something dark. There was a wine bottle on the floor nearby.

"I really don't want to track anything in," Reggie said.

"It could only be an improvement."

"Still," and she slid off her muddy sneakers, held them in one hand, before she stepped inside. She jumped a little when she heard Denny close the door behind her. It sounded oddly final.

He reached for the TV remote he'd left on his chair and switched off the TV. "I like the animal stuff," he said, nodding at the blank screen. "I watch some of these things and sometimes I get the feeling people are the only animals that can't get along with each other." Then, "Pizza?" he offered. "It's cold but there's a microwave in the kitchen that sorta works; I can heat it up."

She shook her head. "Gave up on the Clipper?"

"Variety is the spice of life. Chicago spoiled me. Diamond Cove only has one pizzeria -- *one* -- and they don't deliver. Barbarians."

"Savages." She almost smiled; the little bit of banter reminded her of their time in Portland.

"Still, since half the town lives in places like this tucked in the woods, I get it. I wouldn't deliver either...and I carry a gun. Have a seat." He gestured toward the little sofa.

Still holding her sneakers, she walked across the worn wall-to-wall that had obviously come with the trailer and sat. "I didn't come to apologize for tonight, Denny."

"Just to lay me out like Alan Danning?"

"Well, him I might owe an apology. I just can't seem to work up to it, though." A quick smile between them, but then, "I had to speak up for Frank."

Denny nodded. He hadn't moved from his place by the door, keeping the room between them. "I get it. Professional ethics. Maybe *I* should apologize. I lost my temper; I was out of line. It's not like I don't know how confidentiality works. I guess it's just this business getting to me --"

"I *had* to say something!" She hadn't meant to blurt it out like that.

"Ok," Denny said, calming.

She nodded at the glass on the TV table. "What're you drinking?"

Denny picked up the wine bottle from the floor. "Jonathan gave me this when I hired on. He said it was a house-warming thing, but I think he just wanted to show off his connoisseur chops. See?" and he held the bottle up for her to see. "Fancy! No screw top!"

It was hard not to smile. "What is it?"

"I don't know, some cabernet de snooty bullshit."

"I'm not acquainted with that vintage. I wouldn't mind a taste."

He disappeared into the kitchen, came out with another water glass, poured her a splash, and handed the glass to her.

"I love your stemware."

Denny clinked the bottle against her glass, toast-like. "Came with the place. Everything did. And the place came with the job."

"They're really spoiling you," she said wryly.

"Yeah. I haven't seen the need to --. Well, you're the first company I've ever had here."

She drained her glass. "Jonathan does know his wine." She held the glass out to him. "Can I get a little more of that cabernet de snotty bullshit?"

"*Snooty* bullshit."

"Ah, snooty bullshit."

He poured her a couple of fingers, freshened his own drink, and sat in the farthest chair. "Ok, so you came out here *not* to apologize. So why *did* you come out here?"

She took a sip of the wine. If felt warm and silky going down. Jonathan Manx really *did* know his wine. "I like you Denny," she said, losing her gaze in her glass, unable to look Denny in the eye. "But when you're in the wrong, I'm going to call you out on it. I have to."

"I said, I understand. Confidentiality --"

"It's more than that." She drained her glass, again, and she realized that door she'd been reluctant to open was beginning to swing wide. "You told me why you became a policeman. I owe it to you to tell you how I became a psychologist."

"You don't owe me anything, Reggie."

"Well, let's say I want to tell you, ok?" And for some reason she couldn't reach with her professional analyst's tools, she *did* want to tell him; felt *compelled* to tell him.

"The floor is yours."

Reggie slumped against the back of the sofa. "My father wanted a son. And he never stopped reminding me of that. 'My business isn't the kind of business you leave to a girl,'" and she imitated her father's gruff growl. "That's how he always put it: 'My business doesn't go to a *girl*.'"

"Well, that's a lot of dads, isn't it? A son to carry on the name and all that stuff."

She made a hand motion for him to hold off on a judgment just yet. "My father was a self-made man. Started out just a laborer, ten years later he was building houses with his own company. He was smart -- about his business -- driven, and he did know his trade. Like a lot of self-made men, he didn't credit any of his success to luck, opportunity. It was all about *him*, and he made sure to let you know it. And also like a lot of self-made men, it wasn't enough for him to keep bragging about his success; he had to make sure you knew he thought *you* were a failure. *You* were lazy, stupid...weak.

"He was big on hurting people that way, cutting them down. Even my mother. If she stood up to him, he yelled her down for defying him. And when she got tired of fighting with him and gave up, he despised her for her weakness.

"So, some nickel-and-dime Freud here: if my father wanted to spend his life hurting people, the best way I could get back at him was to spend mine helping people. Healing them."

"I'm guessing he didn't think much of you becoming a psychologist."

She held her empty glass out, again, and Denny crossed the room to pour her another three fingers. This time he sat in the near chair.

Reggie took a sip of the wine. She closed her eyes against a memory that, all these years later, still pained her. "He thought it was nothing more than babysitting -- his words -- a bunch of whiners and crybabies."

"Even when you started treating policemen?"

"*Especially* policemen. 'What'd they think they were signing on for?'" -- the imitated growl again -- "'Just to write parking tickets and be crossing guards for schoolkids?' As far as he was concerned, I wasn't helping anyone, just coddling them."

Denny shook his head, sighing. "What a prince."

Reggie sat quietly for a long moment, appreciating that Denny didn't push, didn't nudge. She looked over at him and he gave a little smile signaling he'd be as patient as she needed him to be.

You've come this far, she told herself, drained her glass yet again, and quietly said, "Have you ever had to use your gun?"

"I've been lucky," he said, sounding relieved. "Only ever had to draw it twice, never had to drop the hammer."

Reggie nodded, as relieved for him as he seemed to be for himself. She took a deep breath, then, "Oliver Chisom."

She'd said it so quietly, Denny hadn't quite heard. "Who…?"

Reggie firmed up. "Oliver Chisom," she said, now loud and clear.

"And who is Oliver Chisom?"

Reggie felt her eyes begin to sting. "One of my policemen. Eleven-year veteran. On a day off, he walked into a convenience store to buy a soda, walked into the middle of a robbery. The perp took a shot at him, Ollie drew his off-duty pistol and -- …" She shook her head as if that would shake off the chill she now felt coursing through her body. "It was a clean shoot. Witnesses, ballistics report, everything -- *everything* -- said Ollie was justified."

Denny nodded, understanding, seeming to already sense where this was going. "Even a clean shoot can take a toll."

"Especially when the perp is a fourteen-year-old kid. So, Ollie took some heat for quite a while. Kid's family, family's lawyer, the press, 'Couldn't you have just winged him?' You know how it goes."

"I've seen the dynamic."

She looked off, past the walls of the trailer, back to the campus and the conference room and a self-punishing Frank Cole. "I know what Frank's going through with that Broder kid. You get patients, they're very good at saying what you want to hear. 'How're you doing?' 'Oh, I'm fine, I'm feeling better every day, I think

I'm past it, thanks, Doc.' They hide it from you. I'm not sure why. Funny; I think maybe they don't want to disappoint you. But they hide it, and they're good at hiding it. Later, you still think if you were any good at your job, you'd've seen the signs."

"What happened to him?" But Denny seemed to already know.

"He came in for a session, told me it was his last one, he felt fine, didn't need to see me anymore. 'Thanks, Doc.'" She looked down at the hand Ollie Chisom had shaken before he had left her office that afternoon. "'Thanks, Doc.'" Then, angry: "Thanks for *what?*" She held out her glass.

"No," Denny said. "I think you've had enough."

She reached for the bottle he had set by the chair, but he grabbed it and pulled it away, holding it out of reach.

She nodded; fine. "Ollie Chisom went home, downed half a bottle of cheap scotch, and put his gun in his mouth."

They sat quietly for a moment. Reggie felt the tears sliding down her cheeks.

Denny reached over with the bottle of wine and poured her a few fingers. "I'm gonna guess your father was less than sympathetic."

She laughed caustically, again falling into her dad's berating, animalistic growl: "'See? I told you, you weren't doing these whiners any good!'" She took a pull on her glass, sunk a little lower into the sofa with a sigh. "And it was hard not to think maybe he was right."

"We're not plumbers, Reggie. We don't plug a hole and twist a wrench and everything's fixed. Not every case gets solved, not if you're a cop, not if you're a shrink, hell, not if you investigate plane crashes. Some mysteries stay mysteries."

She smiled wryly and tapped her temple. "Up here, intellectually, I know that. Just like you know it's not proper police procedure to pound wrongdoers. But our heads don't always run the show, do they?"

He nodded, lost in his own thoughts now, but then looked at her with eyes sympathetic and soft. "Sometimes it's not a bad thing when the heart takes over."

"That's a little gooey, isn't it?"

"So's this."

He stood, took her glass out of her hand, set it on the floor, then took her by both hands and brought her to her feet. He was taller than her by a head but as he eased her close to his body, she felt it a natural fit. She looked up through her still tear-blurred eyes, saw him looking down with those soft, soft eyes, then his lips were on hers; gently at first, barely a peck, then a brushing of lips against lips, and then finally, committedly, pressed firm. She pulled him tight and close, and all the reservations she'd had on the drive over, all the reservations she'd had for years fell away.

He parted just enough to take her by the hand, walking her as he might walk with her along a path in the park, to the dark bedroom at the far end of the trailer. He stopped them in the narrow doorway, looked down at her as if asking for permission. She reached a hand behind his head, pulled his lips back down to hers, hard, then, unsure of who was responsible, the two fell on the unmade bed.

Chapter Eight

Reggie had lain awake in the dark for some time, listening to Denny's easy breathing, his body nestled close to hers. She had made her decision as soon as her eyes had fluttered open, not looking forward to its execution, but submitting to it with the same grim resignation of anyone who sees the necessity of some sort of surgery, of an amputation.

She slid quietly out of the bed, freezing when she thought she'd disturbed him. He stirred slightly under the sheets, but once he resettled, she scooped her clothes off the floor, closed herself in the trailer home's closet-sized bathroom and began pulling on her clothes.

She tried not to look at herself in the mirror, but catching a glimpse was inevitable in the small space, and it held her. What're you doing? she asked herself. She was good enough at her job to know why, but like her most frustrating patients, the knowing didn't stop her. Like she'd told Denny the night before: the head doesn't always run the show.

After she dressed, she considered slipping outside to her car and heading home, but in the stillness of the trailer, she could hear Denny's deep, peaceful breathing. The sound stopped her as she reached for the front door:

Chickenshit! she told herself. She owed him more than that. Or maybe, she thought, she didn't want to live with the idea that that was how she'd left him.

She sat on the small sofa where she had parked the night before, sunk in the lumpy cushions, worried she might slip off to sleep at the same time she was nowhere close to it, wired, waiting for the conversation she didn't want to have, needed to have.

The night turned to the gray of predawn outside, she could hear the chirps and twittering's of morning birds, and then the rustling of sheets from the bedroom.

"Reggie?" More alarmed: "Reggie!"

"I'm here, Denny."

A moment later he was standing there in the half-light of the living room. He'd pulled on a pair of shorts, and Reggie saw a paper bag in one of his hands. With a pang she recognized it as the bag from the Old Port souvenir shop they'd stopped at yesterday. More painful to her was the smile she could make out on his face, even in the gray light.

"I thought you'd left!" he said, almost chuckling with relief. He held out the bag. "Ya know, you left these in the car yesterday. I'm not surprised with everything that happened --" Then his face froze as he caught her look, and his smile quickly faded, the hand with the bag fell to his side. "You've got that we've-got-to-talk look. I got that same look from my wife before the divorce papers came."

She looked down at her hands, knotting together in her lap. "It's not…like that."

"Ok," he said and dropped heavily into the far chair, where the open pizza box and its half-eaten cold pizza still sat nearby on a TV tray. "What *is* it like?"

"I like you, Denny."

"You told me that last night. How come now you make that sound like bad news?"

"Look, let's be realistic about last night. We've been spending a lot of time together, in stressful situations, we're both in a new place, we'd been drinking --"

"Stop waltzing around, Reggie," he said coldly, "We're both grownups."

She nodded, realizing she was just trying to avoid getting to the final line. "I just want to slow down, that's all."

"How slow is 'slowing down'?"

She shrugged.

"Do you even know what you mean by that?"

"Denny -- ..." But she had no answer.

"I told you why I became a cop, you told me why you became a shrink. You asked me if I'd ever been married, and I told you. Ok, so now it's your turn: what about you?"

She looked away, and when she spoke, she could hear the weakness in her voice. "This is a digression, Denny, and it's not helping either of --"

"Jesus, is this what you do when you get scared? You become the cold, analytical shrink? Answer me: were you ever married? Simple question, Reg, what's the big deal?"

She shook her head and finally bled out a feeble, "No."

"Ever come close?"

"Denny, I just want to --"

"Yeah, slow down, I got that, but I don't think that's it at all. You don't want to slow down. You want out and I'll be damned if I can figure out why."

And now Reggie was angry, not because Denny was pressing her, but because he was too close to being on target. She abruptly got to her feet and started for the door. "I'll call you."

He nodded, clearly not believing her.

"I mean it, Denny," and left, not sure she believed it either.

The morning was still gray when Reggie pulled up to Ann Bonano's house. She was surprised to see Ann not only awake, but inside the open barn doors of the studio, apparently doing something to the frame of a claw-footed wooden chair set on some stacked wooden crates. Reggie climbed out of her car and as she drew close, she saw the chair had no cushion, no fabric, and Ann was applying uneven dabs of paint to the naked woodwork with a sponge creating an attractive, calculatedly age-mottled look.

"You're up early," Reggie said.

"Haven't been to bed. It's nice when you don't have to work for a living. You don't have to live on everybody else's twenty-four-hour cycle. I just keep going until I start to hallucinate." Ann gave a quick glance at Reggie, grinned slightly before turning back to her work. "Am I looking at the walk of shame? Or buyer's remorse? Or belated Christian guilt?"

"Maybe all three," Reggie sighed.

"The morning after is a hell of a time to start thinking it was a mistake."

"I'm not sure it was. I'm not sure it wasn't."

"Oh, boy," Ann said, shaking her head, "One of those."

Reggie looked back down along the shore of the cove toward the cluster of rocks, remembering seeing Denny there the night of her dinner with Jonathan Manx and Frank Cole at the Clipper, smoking his Cole-banned cigarette. Her eyes moved from there to the lulling, soothing sight of the cove's waters, and she understood why some people wanted to live by the sea. "I'm just not sure it was the best thing for either of us." She turned back to Ann. "What're you doing?"

"Most people in this town don't have the money for new furniture. Sometimes they just don't want to give up a piece that's been in the family, sometimes for a couple of generations. I make a few dollars doing restorations. Who says artistic skills are a waste?" She finished her dabbing, tossed the sponge down in the pan of paint at her feet, stepped back to regard her handiwork. "At a certain point in your life, sweets, everybody has picked up enough dings and dents that nobody's going to be perfect."

"I know; everybody has their demons."

Ann nodded with theatrical exaggeration at the chair. "As she points unsubtly to the obvious symbol of the restored chair, the old bat sagely counsels the young lady from the big city, you can't make anything new again, but you can get it into a shape where it's nice to have around."

"This from the lady who spends her nights alone getting half-crocked." Reggie winced, immediately regretting having said it. "I'm sorry. That was cruel."

"And inaccurate," Ann said, waving it away. "I never get just *half*-crocked. And if you don't want to end up the same way, don't throw out a perfectly good chair just because the upholstery needs redoing. And, yes, I know I'm beating the analogy to death. You want some breakfast?"

"I don't have time, but --" Reggie shifted on her feet, for the moment unsure of what she did want.

"Mama Anna Banana knows what you want," Ann said and gathered Reggie in her arms for a close, comforting hug.

Reggie felt herself releasing an easing breath, her own arms going around Ann. "Maybe *you* should be the shrink."

"Not a good idea," Ann said as they separated. "I have a tendency to lump people into just two groups: the ones who need a hug, and those who need a spanking."

"I'm fine with just the hug."

"Go clean up, go to work, make Mama proud."

For the first time that morning, Reggie found herself smiling.

Reggie took a quick shower, slid into some slacks and a light pullover, then drove to the campus. It was still early, only a few students poking about, stumbling to the cafeteria in the early morning haze of young people who, away from mommy and daddy for the first time, stayed up too late, ate too much junk food, and probably indulged in a bad habit or two as well. It was hard for Reggie not to smile as some young people passed close by, their clothes infused with the fragrant aroma of marijuana.

It was early enough that she was the first one into her building. She fumbled around for the switch to the corridor lights, then, her arms filled with the texts and manuals she'd been assigned for the semester, went through more fumbles to get her office keys out of her pocketbook.

And then saw she wouldn't need her keys.

Her office door was slightly open, the office mostly dark, below the bar of morning sun coming in through the high-set windows. She found the light switch.

"Jesus!"

She dropped her books and stepped back. But then shock gave way to anger.

Inside her office was the plush puffin and moose Denny had bought her the day before, only the cloth skins had been ripped open and their stuffing thrown around the office.

Reggie had often noted the paradox of being afraid of her feelings, but not of threatening situations. In the same way her father had taught her to land a punch, he'd also tempered her, hammered at her in his search for a son in his daughter the way an armorer hammered steel into a broadsword. She scooped up the stuffing and deflated bodies of the plushies, jammed them into the souvenir shop bag that had been left on the floor and stormed back to her car.

It was only a few minutes' drive to the police station, and she felt a grim satisfaction in seeing that Denny's SUV was parked out front. She bumped up against the curb, slammed her car into park, and without bothering to kill the engine or even close her door behind her, charged toward the door that led to the police department offices.

Little Grace Whitney, apparently having just arrived on the job, had yet to slip off her jacket. She was just setting a take-out cup of coffee on the desk when Reggie exploded through the door. "Good morning, Dr. McLaren. I think the chief –"

But Reggie barely noticed her. She could see beyond Whitney through the open door into Denny's office, see him sitting over a take-out container of something or another for breakfast. *This psycho fucker can eat breakfast after what he pulled this morning?* Reggie screamed in her head.

He must've heard her coming, looked up from his breakfast, started to rise from his chair, obviously not knowing what to make of the way she was coming at him.

She stopped in the doorway of his office and flung the bag at his head. Denny ducked slightly and the bag sailed by.

"*You fucking child!*" she hissed.

"Reggie, what --"

"I know this is a small town, but you better work goddamn hard at seeing we don't cross paths, because I swear to Christ, you come anywhere in reach of me, and I *will* lay you out!"

She spun around, stormed out the same way she'd charged in. She saw Grace Whitney had fallen into her desk chair, eyes wide, mouth an aghast little "o," and Reggie took a sense of victory from the effect she was having. "Happy now, Dad?" and realized with surprise she'd said it out loud.

By the time Reggie was pulling into the parking lot behind the Computer Sciences building, she felt completely drained. Part of it was that she'd hardly had a full night's sleep since that night at the Clipper when she'd first met Denny Petit, but then the white-hot anger over Denny's infantile stunt with the plush toys had burned through whatever store of energy she might have had.

But that wasn't all.

She was still angry at Denny, pissed as hell she told herself, but the hot burning phase was over, and in the fall-off that came after the catharsis came…the sadness. She had connected with Denny, felt it down at Casco Bay, felt it even more strongly last night when she'd opened up to him in a way she had never opened up to anyone before -- even herself. And now?

When she'd left Denny that morning, Denny was right that she was being dishonest with both him and herself when she'd talked about calling him, but still… She had been telling herself, even if it was more self-deception than truth, that whatever was between them was still there, waiting to be picked up when she was ready. But between Denny's pettiness of tearing up the plush toys and certainly with her own furious counterattack, it sank in with a brutal bluntness that that bridge had been burned, blown up, and washed away.

And what moved her to the brink of tears was that it was all her fault. If she hadn't walked away that morning...

Her fatigue, the psychological and physical drag on her, were enough that she would have liked nothing more to sit in her car and let the sobs come, but there were students about, crisscrossing the campus, some of whom were, in a few days, going to wind up in her classrooms. She gathered herself together, pulled herself out of the car and headed for the Computer Sciences entrance.

Inside, alone in the corridor where the Psychology Department offices were, out of sight of the rest of the campus, she let herself sag, her mock-confident stride becoming a tired trudge. The shuffle of papers was a clear sound in the empty hallway. She saw her office door was open, then remembered she hadn't closed it when she'd run off to confront Denny.

Then she was in the doorway, looking down at Frank Cole on his knees gathering up her books and manuals.

"Frank?"

He looked up, his face first going to surprise, then laughing relief. "Reggie? Oh, boy, lady, you won't believe how you scared the crap out of me this morning. I came in, saw the open door, then all this stuff on the floor, and with what's been going on around here the last few days, well, you can imagine where my head went!"

"Let me help you with that."

And now he frowned. "Jesus, Reggie, you look like hell. I've got this." He gathered the mess on the floor into a pile and shoveled it into her still-empty bookcase. "Why don't you sit down."

"I'm ok."

"Like hell. Sit down before you fall down." He took her by the hand and led her to her chair.

She dropped heavily into her desk chair. Cole stepped back, leaning against a far wall, giving her as much space as the small office would allow. He waited.

He's good, she thought, and knew he was seeing her go through the same push-pull of most of her patients: needing the catharsis of talking a situation out, but not wanting to face it. She was a good enough analyst -- though, she admitted, a lousy patient -- to know the healthy route to choose.

"I spent last night with Denny."

"I presume you don't mean a casual sleepover of horror movies and pillow fights."

She tried not to grin, but she appreciated Cole's way of trying to defuse the angst. "You know what I mean."

"And then morning comes, and in the cold light of day, you had second thoughts and told him this was all too much too soon."

"Not exactly a novel pattern, I admit."

"Well, let's just say you wouldn't be the first to experience Morning After Syndrome. And then?"

Reggie told him about finding the plush toys Denny had bought her mangled and strewn around her office, then storming over to Denny's office and --

Cole held up a halting hand. "Come with me." She followed him to his office, took his invitation of the cushy guest chair, watched curiously as he checked to make sure the outside hall was empty, locked his office door, then sat in his desk chair, pulled out his key chain and found the small key for one of his locked desk drawers. "I am swearing you to secrecy, Reggie. Swear!"

Reggie crossed her heart and touched her index finger to her lips.

"Don't tell anybody about this," Cole said as he pulled the bottom drawer open. "I'm not supposed to have this on campus." He pulled out a small bottle of brandy and two small paper cups from a stash in the drawer. "I keep it for some of my more overwrought student clients which I'm not supposed to do, either."

"Isn't it a bit early in the day?"

"This isn't recreational. This is medicinal." He poured them each a healthy shot in the cups, then handed one to Reggie. They raised their cups in salute. "I apologize for the quality, but on what they pay here -
-"

Reggie took a healthy sip and gasped.

"See what I mean?"

She finished her cup anyway. "Big step down from your practice in Philadelphia?"

Cole belted his dose down with only some mild wincing. "About the same, actually. I never had a private practice. I always worked in the city's Behavioral Health

Division. Public worker's pay, I didn't do much better than this."

"A do-gooder. God, my father would've hated you!"

"What does that mean?"

"For another time."

Cole nodded, agreeing. He looked into his empty cup for a moment, then turned to her. "Denny didn't do it. Your office. That wasn't him."

"I know you're his friend, Frank --"

"He called me right after you left his place this morning, we met for coffee, we talked. He had those toys, dolls, whatever you call them, he had them with him. They were still intact, by the way."

"How do you know he didn't leave your little chat and then come by my office --"

"Because he called me not long before you got here to tell me what happened at his office with you, and to ask me if I knew what the hell was going on. He thinks *you* tore them up."

"He's lying."

"Why would he lie?"

"I don't know. To get you on his side. To, to, to…" But Reggie couldn't find a good reason.

"I know my track record of late hardly recommends me," Cole said, and the way his face suddenly clouded Reggie knew he was referring to poor Andy Broder, "but I'll stake my license on my believing he didn't do this. When I talked to him, Reggie, he wasn't angry. He wasn't even angry when you threw that stuff at him. If I had to describe his emotional state, I think the unscientific word I'd use is, 'heartbroken.'"

Reggie turned away, not wanting to show she was feeling something at least not too dissimilar. "You saying I should go back?"

"I didn't say that Reg."

She shook her head. "What *are* you saying? You're confusing me, Frank. First you seem like you're pushing us together --"

"Purely for therapeutic reasons…for *both* of you."

"I don't think last night was therapeutic for either of us."

"While I'm not tickled at the turn it's taken, I still might disagree."

"But weren't you also telling me -- just *yesterday* -- to be careful?"

"I know. I'm a conundrum." Grinning broadly, Cole spread out his arms. "'Do I contradict myself? Very well, then, I contradict myself. I am large --'"

"'I contain multitudes,' yeah, I know, I had English Lit, too."

Cole went serious. "We've had three murders and a suicide in one weekend. Right now, I'd tell anybody to be careful around *anybody*, be it the chief of police, me, Jonathan Manx, crazy Ann Bonano, the creepy guy who mops down the halls at night -- you haven't met him yet and you'll wish you hadn't when you do. My point is until we get a handle on what's going on, I'll tell you what I'd tell anybody: be careful alone, spend most of your time in public places. For all I know, Denny Petit is Jack the Ripper resurrected. But he didn't do *this* is all I'm saying." Then he paused, frowning in thought. "You know…"

"What?"

"You might have to consider the possibility of a third party."

"Like whom?"

"Well, I haven't done any work in criminal forensics, but it strikes me that if you can figure out the *why*, that leads you to *who*. And the *why* that leaps immediately to mind is jealousy."

"Well, if that's the case and that's the motive, wouldn't you be the obvious *who*?"

Cole smiled. "Yes, and I've very cleverly concealed my secret desire for you by nudging you toward my romantic nemesis. Look, it may not even be that kind of jealousy. Someone jealous of your position, your situation --"

"My what?"

"C'mon, Reggie, give yourself some credit. You're young, attractive, smart, with a position that gives you what passes for top-tier status in Diamond Cove."

Reggie had never been comfortable with compliments and now felt it her turn to break a mood. She pulled her shoulders up coquettishly, blinked her eyes like a bad actress, and in a squeaky voice said, "Tell me more about my eyes!"

Cole laughed. "Have you had breakfast? C'mon, I'll get you something to eat."

"Is this a date, Frank?"

Frank Cole laughed again.

While Reggie had asked half-jokingly, the half that hadn't been a joke couldn't tell what kind of answer she'd gotten.

Cole walked Reggie to the Student Center but led her past the cafeteria and its din of chattering students and clattering dishware. "It's not bad…for a cafeteria," Cole said, "but it's *still* a cafeteria."

The Student Center was situated on a slope. Cole led her to a small café-like arrangement downstairs which opened on a small veranda looking out on one of the campus's greens where students lounged in chatting groups or singly with eyes glued to cell phones, or -- in a phenomenon that never ceased to fascinate Reggie -- in silent groups with each member of the clutch fiddling with their phones.

Cole treated them to coffee and some breakfast wraps, and they sat at one of the garden tables on the veranda.

"Remember when you mentioned the Manhattan Study to Jonathan the other night? Their finding that whoever wasn't getting help, either needed help or *would* need help?"

Reggie mumbled a "Yes" through a mouthful of scrambled eggs and bacon bits.

"Between what I saw in Philly at Behavioral Health and even what I've seen with my student clients in the short time I've been here, it's hard -- *damned* hard -- not to think every one of them --" and Cole nodded out at the students on the green "-- is damaged somehow."

"Well, when that's all you deal with day after day --"

"I know, I know, it skews your view, it's hardly a scientific sample. But one bruised soul after another comes into your office..." Cole shook his head, put down his wrap, his face clouded.

"You're thinking about Andy Broder," Reggie said softly.

"You saw his parents."

Reggie sighed in sad agreement. "Even in just that brief glimpse, I get it. It was almost textbook: pushy dad, muzzled mom." And to herself, Reggie was thinking, I get it because I lived the same scenario.

"But here's the thing," Cole went on, "if...what happened hadn't happened, if I wasn't able to...*heal* Andy, and he'd gone on to have kids of his own, somehow, in some way, it would've come out at his *own* kids; maybe not the same way he'd been hurt, maybe even not meaning to hurt his own kids, but he would've passed it on, almost like a genetic flaw. And his kids would've done the same to theirs, and on and on.

"And you can reverse engineer it. Andy's parents were the way they were because they'd been damaged by *their* parents, and back and back and back until you get to Adam and Eve and telling them how they screwed up their kids and that's why Cain took a club to his brother."

His face had grown darker as he'd spoken, his voice a developing mix of sadness and anger.

"You see so much...*stuff* come through your door," he said after a pause, "it makes you wonder whether it's even possible to break those chains."

It was not an alien concern to Reggie, and she was sure that, at one time or another, every analyst wondered the same thing...even without a father actively fostering the idea it was always a futile exercise. "But you stay with it," Reggie said, although it was as much her looking for an answer as offering support.

Cole smiled. "So do you. Ever wonder why?"

It was her turn to smile. "Constantly." After pondering the thought for a few moments, "Maybe… Maybe because it's better than doing nothing."

It was both unsatisfying yet answered the question for both. They both smiled at that and that was enough to send Cole back to his food.

"About Denny," Reggie said, and Cole comically rolled his eyes. "What should I do?"

Cole put on a mock-serious face, playing the heavy caliber analyst: "Hmm, interesting question. What do *you* think you should do?"

"I hate when shrinks do that," Reggie said wryly. "Even when *I* do it."

Cole finished off the last bite of his wrap, glanced at his watch, then drained his coffee and stood. "I have a meeting with some IT nerds to get my office computer wired up. Oooh, I shouldn't call them nerds; that was very unprofessional of me! Later, Reggie."

As he started off, Reggie called after him: "About that dinner. You know; the collegial one where we discuss departmental matters?"

Cole smiled but with a sad touch to it. "You're just trying to push Denny behind you, Reggie. Let the smoke settle first, and then we'll see. I'd hate to wind up just the first bounce on a rebound."

She felt herself blushing with the truth of it. "Rain check, then."

Cole made a pistol of his fingers and sent an imaginary shot her way: "Rain check," and then he headed off.

"Hey, Frank!" Reggie called, nagged by a late thought.

Cole stopped and turned.

"You said when you talked with Denny this morning, he had the plushies with him and they were still in one piece. They didn't walk off by themselves and commit ugly suicide in my office."

"I told him to throw them out. I told him they'd only be an unhappy reminder of this morning."

Reggie nodded and Cole turned, again, to leave, but Reggie called out again: "How do you know that's what he did?"

"I presume he did."

"How do you *know?*"

Cole gave her a small, tolerant smile. "Like I told you; on *this*, I trust him."

As she took her evening jog, Reggie gave The Clipper a wide berth, not wanting to bump into Denny or, for that matter, after being embarrassingly called out that afternoon, Frank Cole. Remembering finding Denny propped on the rocks on the beach along the cove, she avoided the beach as well. It was well dark by the time she was heading for home. As she neared Ann Bonano's house, she saw, silhouetted against the glints of moonlight off the bay, a slumped figure sitting on the steps at the end of Ann's walk that led down to the beach. The figure sat upright at the sound of her footfalls, and she instantly recognized the close-cropped head, the broad shoulders, caught a glimpse of moon glitter off the badge on his chest. She abruptly slowed to a walk, unsure if she should be angry…relieved…or afraid.

Denny stood, held up his two hands as if surrendering. "Don't get mad."

"I'm not mad." And it was only after she'd said it, she realized it was true. "Actually…"

He waited, then, "Yes?"

She took a few steps closer. "Actually, I'm thinking I -- …"

"Yes?"

She took a few more steps, not wanting to close the distance, but finding herself unable to keep it. "I'm thinking I owe you an apology."

"You don't --"

She held up a hand to quiet him. "For this morning. I thought you were the one who, well… You know."

"And now you don't?"

"I talked to Frank --"

Even in the dark she could see Denny shaking his head. "Jesus, for a guy who talks a good game about confidentiality --"

"I believe him."

"I'm glad." Denny was quiet for a moment. He looked out at the waters of the cove, alight with moon-shimmer. He sighed.

"What?"

"Well, if you believe I didn't do it, and I thought it was you and you didn't do it… This just got a little scary.

"A little."

He turned back to her. "Are you ok?"

She shrugged, and he shrugged back.

"Is that why you're here?" she asked, "To talk about this morning?"

"That was part of it. I figured, well, I was thinking about what you said back at my place. I didn't take it too well --"

"You don't have to say anything --"

But he pushed on: "-- and I got to thinking I owe *you* an apology. You know; for pressing like that."

She sat on the steps and didn't move when Denny sat down beside her. "You asked me a question this morning," she said. "You deserve an answer."

"I had no right --"

"Shut up, Denny." She said it with a faint smile, hoping he could see it in the darkness. "I was never married. I was never even close. Whenever things looked like they might develop in that direction...I bailed. Disappointing behavior in a student of the mind, don't you think?"

He sat with that a moment. "I know you're the professional shrink, and I barely passed Psych 101 at a second-rate college, but do you mind if I try some amateur psychology?"

She nodded at him to go ahead.

"Not all men are like your dad."

She slumped a bit, sighed as the heavy truth of it settled on her. But then, she thought, somewhere inside she'd always known that was the truth of it. "Give me some time to get myself to believe that." It wasn't a declaration; it was a quiet request.

"As much time as you need. I said I owed you an apology, too, Reggie. No, I do because you were right: it was too much, too fast. Everything you said, about the time together, throw in too much wine… You were right. We don't really know each other." He stood, then, restless with the energy of it, pacing back and forth then turning back to face the cove, as if drawing some calming solace from the easy roll of the waves lapping quietly at the beach. He nodded his head in acceptance. "You were right. But I'd like to, Reggie; get to know you." He turned toward her. "If you'll let me.

"They have these craft days here on some weekends, people set up tables on the sidewalks, put out their stuff. I'd like to know what it's like to walk through the center of town with you, looking at the things people made with their hands, then stop at their one lousy pizza place for a slice and joke with you about how these people don't know what good pizza is. I want to know what it's like to go to a movie with you -- we might have to go all the way to Portland to do it -- and sit together, share a bucket of popcorn, pretend to fight over the last handful. I want to know what it's like to have you over for dinner even though the only thing I know how to cook is hot dogs and burgers on a barbecue and I'm bad at *that*, and you'd make fun of me for burning everything. I want to know what it's like to sit here on this beach with you, doing nothing but holding your hand while we watch the sun go down.

"I'll take as long as you want to get to know you like that, Reg, and for you to know me. I'll go as slow as you want to go. But you have to let me."

Reggie's eyes stung, she rubbed at them hoping it would look like she was just tired instead of wiping away the wetness. Then she was on her feet, standing in front of Denny. As close as she was standing to him, she was still unable to clearly see his face in the dark. She didn't know how long they were standing there. It could've been just seconds. It could've been forever.

"This is where you're supposed to kiss him, dumbass!" came Ann Bonano's voice from her perch on her deck above them.

Denny bent down, but only partway, tentative, waiting to see if he was welcome. Reggie tilted her head back and went up on her toes. It was a long but gentle kiss. This wasn't passion; this was something deeper than passion.

Then Denny stepped back and gave her a light peck on her forehead. "Slow," he said, accepting. "And start locking your door at night."

Reggie sensed more than saw a smile on his face and stayed standing at the foot of the steps as Denny turned and walked off down the beach. She stayed there until his broad form disappeared into the night.

Then Ann Bonano's voice from above, again, and it was hard for Reggie not to laugh: "C'mon up. It's Tom Collins night."

Even after one too many of Ann Bonano's exceptionally potent Tom Collins', Reggie had trouble sleeping through the night. Several times she would stir from a light and hardly restful sleep to toss in her bed, her head pinballing from one troubling thought to another:

There was, of course, the obvious and understandable fear that a maniac was loose in Diamond Cove and had run up a brutal score of three in just a few days (four if one wanted to count the unfortunate fallout of poor Andy Broder's suicide).

The equally obvious and understandable fear that if Denny Petit and Frank Cole were being truthful, some unknown party had targeted Reggie for some unknown reason which had disturbed Reggie enough to not only take Denny's advice of locking her door that night but wedging one of her mis-matched kitchen chairs under the doorknob.

And the thought that gnawed at her most -- Denny.

His willing patience she found as unnerving as the intimacy of the night before because there was no logical -- scratch that -- no *sane* reason to say no to him…and yet part of her kept declaring *No! No! No!*

Denny had been right -- to a certain extent -- that her inhibitions were about the horror show that had been her parents' marriage. But how many patients had sat in her office talking about relationships gone bad, trusts abused, promises broken? She knew that part of her jaded view was not too dissimilar to those of the policemen she'd treated.

"No one ever calls us to watch someone do good," one of her police officers had told her, and the constant barrage of being exposed to the worst aspects of the human character inevitably cultivated the idea in her cops that *all* people were stamped out of the same cracked and flawed and inherently malevolent mold.

What had paraded through her office, session after session, day after day, had certainly built up a similar sensibility in her head: all people had their demons (I'll give you that one, Ann Bonano!), and all relationships inevitably failed, not by chance and not faultlessly

Intellectually, she knew this wasn't true, but she also knew – at the same intellectual level, oddly enough -- that this wasn't about intellect or logic or rational thinking. This was about seeing her mother humiliated and emotionally beaten down every day of her marriage, and Reggie coming to believe, you only have to make the wrong choice *once!*

Unsurprisingly, then, she was operating in something of a fog as she climbed out of bed, making a great effort at resisting the urge to silence the alarm on her phone and fall back onto the tangled sheets. She fumbled her way through a quick shower, pulled on some clothes, and drove over to the campus. That same fog was why she was only dimly aware of a small fuss across the school's central green, over by the library, where some students were watching a tow truck haul away a car.

Reggie laughed inwardly; is the thrill level that low in Diamond Cove that a car tow draws a crowd? And then she thought, with another silent laugh, Yeah, it probably is!

She trudged lead-footed into the Computer Sciences building. The door to Frank Cole's office was open. She stuck her head in to say hello and froze.

Cole was seated at his desk, slumped in his chair, head tilted over the chair back, his mouth hanging open.

"Oh, God…" She felt her knees start to flex and weaken and grabbed for the doorsill.

Then Cole's chest heaved, and he let out a soft, purring snore.

At which point she couldn't decide if she was angry enough to tilt him out of his chair, or able to step back and laugh at her own paranoias.

She went with a third option which was to walk up to the slumped figure and poke him in the shoulder. "Hey, Frank," she said quietly, then a firmer poke and a firmer voice: "Frank!"

With a gasp and a cough, Frank shot up in his seat. "What the hell --?" He rubbed his eyes and squinted with bloodshot orbs up at her. "Reggie?"

"In the flesh."

"Did I fall asleep?"

"Yes, and it's been twenty years, and you've got twenty years' worth of classes wondering when you're going to post their grades."

Cole managed a lazy smile. He pointed to two take-out coffee cups on his desk. "Have one."

"You bought this for me?"

"No, for me. I needed the caffeine double-header, not that it's doing me any good."

Reggie, feeling she could use a jump-start as well, took one of the cups and sat in Cole's easy chair. She took a sip from the cup and made a face. "Jesus, this is ice cold. How long have you been here?"

Cole squinted at his watch, then gave up trying to read it. "Hell, if I know. It was dark."

"What've you been doing?"

"Denny didn't call you?" The look on her face must've been answer enough: "Guess not."

"I did see him last night."

Cole shook his head, dismissing that for some reason. "I thought maybe… Well, he knows you know more about this kind of thing than I do."

"What kind of --?" And then she got it. "Oh, no" and the one swallow of cold coffee in her stomach turned to ice. "Another one?"

Cole nodded. "Alan Danning,"

"Good Christ."

"They found him in his car parked by the university library."

"Like the others?"

Another nod. "Found the hammer on the floor of the car."

Reggie sat with that for a few seconds. The mental fog lifted, and now everything had a painful clarity to it. "What was he doing by the university library?"

"Well, naturally, the first person Denny talked to was – "

"Marcia Danning."

"She said it wasn't the first time he'd been hanging around there. Sometimes she'd find him sitting in his car on the street where she lives."

"That's a bit unusual, isn't it? Usually, a molester lets go when the kid ages out."

Cole nodded and shrugged, having already made the same considerations. "Maybe we misread him a bit. Maybe this was less classic child molestation than obsession. I know you and Denny thought maybe grandma was working through the son to reconnect with Marcia, but now I'm thinking maybe Alan was working the grandma to work David --"

"To get to Marcia. Which makes her the obvious suspect."

"Or the boy."

"Or…"

"What?"

Reggie looked toward the floor. "I saw Denny almost put Alan Danning through a wall."

Cole frowned, working the idea, then his face opened up and he shook it off. "Doesn't figure."

"How so?"

"Because there's a problem with *all* of them. How do you figure the Broders? There's no connection between them and the Dannings, Denny didn't know them. Nothing connects the Danning killings and the Broders." He took a sip from his own coffee cup, made the same wry face Reggie had made. He yawned, then let his bleary eyes settle on Reggie. "It must've hurt him not to call you over this."

"Hurt me a little, too."

Chapter Nine

The rest of Reggie's day was a deep-dive into academic bureaucracy: paperwork to be filled out at Human Resources, getting cleared for a faculty parking tag for access to the campus lots once the semester officially began, a visit to IT to get and activate her faculty email account, a visit to security to get her faculty ID --

"It's ok to smile for the picture, if you want: we're not Motor Vehicles!"

-- online training sessions to get her certifications on harassment prevention, discrimination, the Family Educational Rights and Privacy Act and records confidentiality, sexual misconduct and Title IX, orientation sessions on how to advise students for their classes (Oh, Jonathan, that wasn't in the job description!), on codes of conduct, ethics, grading, and what to do when a student evidenced signs of psychological distress.

"I recognize that you're a licensed professional psychologist, Dr. McLaren, but there is a protocol we have to follow because of liability considerations."

She wondered if Frank Cole had in mind those liability considerations when he dosed troubled students with a shot of medicinal brandy. But then she wasn't surprised; Cole struck her as someone more interested in helping the hurting rather than abiding by any rule that let sufferers continue to suffer.

The facilitator also granted that, ahem, the present, um, "exceptional circumstances of the day" (that being, Reggie mentally clarified, a head-bashing maniac loose in town) might tempt someone to break protocol, but as understandable as that might be, such a breach could very well result in legal action against the university, the transgressor, and probable suspension and possible loss of job.

Reggie vowed to herself to keep that in mind if a student came banging on her door with a ball peen hammer.

She had to manage all this while trying to shake off her morning fog with regular intermission stops at the school's café to refuel on coffee. But in those interstitial pauses, cutting through the mental haze and the dizzying number of procedures, protocols, and policies getting thrown at her throughout the day, were the facts of Alan Danning's murder...and Denny.

Denny. His promise to go as slow as she wanted, and all those things he saw going with that patient approach, brought with it a feeling of intimacy Reggie hadn't felt even during the night they'd spent together. And out of that intimacy she felt an even greater need to put space between her and Denny.

Why?

She raged at herself for not being able to answer, and likewise raged at Denny for -- as she saw it --pressuring her by paradoxically *not* pressuring her.

The most tedious part of an already tedious day became the last stretch…with Jonathan Manx.

"I know you've been given the syllabus templates and such, the new instructors' orientation and all that, but I do so think we need to sit together to discuss the outline of your classes, make sure we're all on the same page, as it were." And he was insistent that that discussion could be more productive oh, say over coffee at the Student Center café.

"I realize it's hardly a Parisian bistro, but I find it's more conducive to a conversational give-and-take than an office, don't you?"

Not that he was really asking. And the conversation wasn't so much give-and-take as a little bit of talk about her classes and a lot more prattling on about how at his previous posting, his curriculum ideas had been -- at least in his self-aggrandizing eyes -- too "maverick," too "outside the box" for the "geriatric administration" to appreciate and incorporate. That's why he'd leapt at the Diamond Cove opening, not just to finally design a curriculum the way he saw fit, but to "-- and I hate to admit to this kind of pettiness, but to show the old fogies back at that-institution-that-shall-not-be-named that on which they had so blindly missed out."

Manx's self-back-patting soliloquies sometimes went on so long that Reggie, drained by the day and a lack of restorative sleep the night before, found herself zoning out, only to drift back into the not-really-a-conversation to find Manx still so intent on touting his self-assumed brilliance that he hadn't noticed her momentarily glazed look.

Reggie saw the sky beginning to darken outside the café windows.

"Must be getting late," she said with what she hoped was at least a fair performance of being casual as she nodded toward the failing light outside. "I feel like we've covered it all, Jonathan, don't you?" It was, she'd hoped, her polite way of calling an end to Manx's performance.

Without any sense of shame or apology, Manx seemed to detect that he'd run out the clock and gave a small smile and nod. "Nothing we can't cover another time, eh?" which seemed frightfully dripping with the promise of an encore performance. He cast a quick look at the café's wall clock. "Oh, I had no idea of the time! I must've bored you silly!"

Reggie forced a smile. "Hardly. It's all new to me, Jonathan, thank you for taking the time."

"As it is getting on, might I ask if you have dinner plans? I promise; no business conversation!"

Reggie smiled, again, as graciously as she could, and tried un-earnestly to look earnestly disappointed. "Any other time, Jonathan, that would be nice, but I've had a long day, you know --"

Manx leaned forward as if they were sharing a secret. "Ah, yes, the dreaded academic bureaucracy! An intellectual boa constrictor capable of squeezing the life out of anyone! I thoroughly understand, Regina, having had to go through that very same grinding mill myself. Ah, well, another time, then."

Some un-earnest earnest nodding on her part. "Another time."

"Are you heading back to your office?"

"Well, I have to pick up some stuff --"

"Ah, then at least I can enjoy your company a few minutes longer as your escort."

"Um, you really don't have to --"

"I'm going that way myself. I have some paperwork to clear up in my office, and with all that's been going on --" and here a grave frown "-- well, Mother Manx would never forgive me leaving you to fend for yourself under the circumstances."

Reggie's cheeks were beginning to hurt from all the feigned gracious smiling. "Of course. Shall we go?"

Manx's idea of enjoying her company for a few minutes more was to continue his one-sided conversation on the way to the Computer Sciences building, this time a long-winded discourse, spurred by the iffy quality of the café's coffee, on his appreciation for African coffees over South American coffees and it was a shame how limited the local selection was, and... Somewhere in there Reggie found herself drifting off again.

Then they were in the Computer Sciences lobby. The offices and computer labs were dark, the students and rest of the staff having long since left. Reggie was about to give Manx a quick, "See you tomorrow, Jonathan!" and scoot off down the stairwell to her basement office, but then Jonathan held up a finger:

"Do you hear that?"

She stopped.

Manx's finger pointed down the main corridor. Cole and Reggie may have been relegated to their basement cubbies, but as a department head -- even if the department only consisted of three people -- Manx felt he deserved something better and had found an empty office suite tucked in a back corner of the main floor.

From down the empty corridor, Reggie could hear the watery echoes of raised voices. The words were indecipherable, and she couldn't make out the voices…yet something of the familiar tickled at her. Slowly, she started off down the corridor, following the sounds, with a wary Manx a few steps behind.

"I think," Manx said, "it may be coming from my office."

"Were you expecting anybody?"

"No. And I thought I'd locked my door."

For a moment, that stopped Reggie. "Are you sure?"

"Pretty sure. Do you think we should call security?"

From the looks of him, Reggie guessed it must've taken every bit of whatever nerve Jonathan Manx had just to get this far. She had the impression she only had to say, "We should go," and that before she'd have finished the sentence, Manx would've disappeared out the doors.

But what pulled at Reggie was now she could not only pick out words, but there was a recognizable pattern to what she could hear. She started farther down the hall. She could hear Manx tentatively shuffling along behind her, probably -- she guessed -- more out of fear of being left alone than not wanting Reggie to go off by herself.

And then, fairly clearly: *"Tell her, Alicia. This time, she __has__ to hear you. In here, she can't talk you down or ignore you. Tell her."* Manx's voice.

Which intrigued in-the-flesh Manx enough to pick up his pace, even passing Reggie down the hall.

Now, a weak, feminine voice: *"I know I wasn't in your plan. You keep telling me…how much better things would be…how different if…if I hadn't been born."*

Then a pause, and it started over: *"Tell her, Alicia…"*

They turned the corner. At the far end of the hall, the door to Manx's reception office was open, the lights on.

The girl, again: *"If you want to be mad at somebody, shouldn't you be mad at yourself? You made me __hate__ myself!"*

At the reception office door, they could see across the room through the door to Manx's office; see the reflection in the windows across from the office's wall shelves where, among the books, was a television. Reggie now recognized the images along with the voices, and as the voices stopped and re-started, so, too, did the image freeze, rewind, and start over.

Now Manx was angry. He pushed past Reggie into his office. The image on the TV froze. "What the hell're you doing here?" Manx demanded.

"I've been looking at this stuff and wondering the same thing about *you*. I'm thinking maybe you're making little Frankensteins."

It was Denny Petit's voice.

Reggie stepped into the room. Denny was at the far end of the office, slouched back in Jonathan Manx's high-backed leather chair behind his desk. He frowned at Reggie's appearance.

"I didn't think you'd be here," he said quietly.

"Is it going to make a difference?"

Denny seemed to weigh it for a few seconds, then -- sadly -- shook his head. "Thing is, I've got some issues to straighten out with your boss here. It might've been better…if you'd been somewhere else."

"You broke in, didn't you?" Manx said. "I locked this office."

"Yes, you did." Denny turned his eyes toward Manx, and whatever regret he felt over Reggie being there instantly evaporated. "You should talk to your security guys, Jonathan, because anybody with fifteen bucks' worth of hardware who half knows what he's doing can pick any lock in this place."

"Denny, goddammit, don't you know you could lose your job over this?"

Denny's lips curled slowly into a smile, something cruel, and Reggie found herself going cold.

"There's no law here tonight, Jonathan. Just us…in a big, empty building."

"Maybe I should leave," Reggie said.

"Maybe you should close the door," Denny said. "I didn't want you to be here, but…here you are. So… The door, Reg."

For a brief second, she considered dashing out the door, wondering how far she'd get. Resigned, she reached behind her and pulled the office door closed.

Denny gestured with the remote to two deep-cushioned chairs set by a coffee table to one side of the office. "Relax."

She and Manx sat. She could see Manx's face was now sheathed in sweat, and she felt her own face glowing with heat, the moisture forming on her forehead. She looked to Denny, studied his face for some clue as to where this was going. Nothing.

Denny's cold smile widened into a grin. "I was just coming to my favorite part. I've watched this part three times, but I never get tired of it. Got yourself a very angry young lady there, Jonathan." He pushed a button on the remote.

Reggie turned to the TV. The video was the same one Manx had used to illustrate his "inner child" sessions; the one with a student named Alicia. Denny speeded the video to the point where Manx was handing Alicia a plastic baseball bat.

"*...who should you be angry with?*" Manx was saying on the video.

"*Her!*"

"*Who?*"

"*My mother!*"

"*Let it out, Alicia! Let the anger out!*"

And that's when Alicia brought the bat down again and again on a pile of foam blocks as the girl cried, "*I hate you!*"

Denny froze the image on Alicia, the girl's face twisted in rage and pain. "You think you're helping these kids, Jonathan?"

"They've been in denial for years. It builds. When the catharsis comes..."

"Oh, you don't have to tell me! God knows there were times I wanted to pop my dad once or twice. Right,

Reggie? I'll bet you would've liked to lay one on dear ol' Dad a time or two, hm?"

Reggie's throat was tight. In fact, her whole body was rigid. She managed only a bare shrug.

Denny carelessly tossed the remote onto Manx's desk, rocked himself meditatively in the chair, staring up at the ceiling as if musing on a point. "Hey, Jonathan, let me ask your professional opinion on something. I've been doing some reading up, you know, because of this, uh, what would you call it? This 'situation' we have. This business of, oh, what's the word?"

But Reggie knew he knew. He's toying with us, she thought.

"You know," Denny went on, "where in your head, you can separate things…"

"Compartmentalization," Reggie said.

Denny stopped his rocking and fixed Reggie with a stare. "I wasn't talking to you, Dr. McLaren. I was talking to the boss there, Dr. Manx."

Reggie slumped in her chair, a slight nod, conceding she wouldn't interfere again.

"Where were we? Ah!" and that hard smile of Denny's was back. "Compartmentalization. Like, say, the person who's running around cracking skulls, he may not even know he's doing it. That's possible, right, Dr. Manx?"

Manx cleared his throat and Reggie could tell by the strangled quality in his voice that Manx was suffering the same tight throat Reggie had. No doubt he had the same cold fear in the pit of his stomach, the same sense that if he stood and tried to run his legs would go to jelly and he'd be down on the floor.

"So, if I got this right, Doctor -- well, we're friends, right? So, *Doc*, this person could, you know -- *bonk-bonk --*" and he mimed striking with a hammer "-- and go to sleep that night, wake up in the morning, and never know what they've been doing. Like sleep walking."

"Well, not exactly --"

"Like, let's say it was *me.*"

Denny let that hang in the air for a long moment, seemed to be enjoying the discomfort he was creating.

"I mean, you know, just for the sake of argument. I could go home at the end of the day, sack out on my lounge chair, watch a little TV, then go off and do something nasty. Like right now. Like, I might've already been home, nodded off, and tomorrow I won't even remember I was here."

"Denny --" Reggie began but Denny held up a finger to silence her, then pointed toward Manx for a response.

"An intriguing possibility," Manx managed to choke out.

"You bet your ass it is," and at that, Denny reached under the desk, brought up a ball peen hammer and brought the steel ball down on the desk so hard it sounded like a cannon shot, cracking through the polished top, and burying the rounded peen a quarter inch into the solid wood.

Reggie and Manx had both jumped at the sight of the hammer and now she wanted to scream but couldn't, silenced by the steel-hard eyes of Denny Petit.

"You know, even as a cop, I go to buy a weapon, I even just go to buy bullets, I've got to show some kind of ID. But these things?" Denny waved the hammer around in front of him. "They don't even look at your face. Pay cash at the hardware store, not even a record of the purchase. Nine ninety-five, Doc, that's all it cost; they were having a sale. Nine ninety-five, and someone stops walking the planet."

Slowly, Denny got to his feet, and just as slowly, with the hammer clenched in one fist, started walking around the desk toward Manx. "Scared, Jonathan? Starting to think about dying? Thinking about what it's going to feel like? Is it going to hurt? Are you really, really scared?"

He was standing in front of Manx, his shadow falling across Manx's face. Reggie could see Denny's fingers flexing around the handle of the hammer.

"Denny," she squeaked out, "Please --"

"I told you to be quiet, Reg," he said. "Well, Jonathan? How's it feel?"

"Bad."

"Good." Denny dropped the hammer on the floor, stepped back and propped himself against the front of Manx's desk. "I don't want to hear any more shit about confidentiality, or what the law says you can and can't tell me --"

Reggie and Manx had both gone slack when the hammer had hit the floor, both simultaneously realizing with the same heavy exhalation, that -- in Denny Petit's words -- they'd be able to walk the planet the next day. But now anger -- no, *rage* -- was boiling up in Manx.

"You come in here like this, you pull this, this...*stunt* --"

"Four people are *dead*, my friend!" Denny shot back. "And from what I saw from your little TV show, I think whoever did it came out of *here!* Karen Danning was being treated here, right? And that Broder kid?"

"I couldn't even confirm they were clients here," Manx said, and then it was his turn to smile evilly: "But I'll tell you this, *my friend;* neither of them was treated through my program!" He pointed at the TV. "Neither of them went through that process!"

"Andy Broder is in that video. He was sitting in that circle."

"He did not go through the cathartic process. He didn't have the breakthrough."

"Breakthrough? That's what you call it?" Denny came close to laughing, then his face went hard again. "I want to see their files."

"I *can't!* I've already been talking to the dean, our lawyers, it's been referred to Augusta --"

"*Fine!*"

Reggie saw Denny's fists ball so tight the knuckles went white. She remembered the time at the Danning house, Denny and Alan Danning, and wondered if she'd be able to stop Denny if he went after Manx the same way.

But Denny closed his eyes tight, seemed to be forcing control over himself, then suddenly went still with a sort of calm. He took a deep breath, his fists opened, his eyes opened. "The next person who dies, Jonathan, my friend, I want you to remember what happened tonight, so you'll know what it was like for them; you'll know the fear they had. And when it happens -- and it *will* happen --I'm leaving the body on your doorstep and giving the next of kin your phone number. You can explain to *them* about confidentiality."

He started for the door, stopped to turn to Reggie. She knew what he was thinking, she could see it on his face: If I'd ever had a chance, I blew it up tonight. "I'm…sorry, Reg. I really didn't want you here for this."

He left and closed the door behind him.

Reggie sank into her chair, drained.

But Manx was storming around the office, fuming. "He thinks this is the way I want it? He thinks I'm happy about this? This is going to destroy the program!"

"That's your concern? The program?"

But Manx didn't seem to hear her. "First thing tomorrow, I'm on the phone with the president and the mayor. Friend or no friend, I'll have his job!"

Reggie pulled herself tiredly out of her chair. "No, you won't, Jonathan."

"The hell I won't!" He stopped his roaring around the office, fixing on an idea: "Not my place to say, Regina, I'd understand if you have feelings for the man, but I can't let that --"

"You won't have him fired, Jonathan," she said, reaching for the door, not caring one way or the other about what Manx thought about her and Denny.

"And why won't I?"

"Because he's right; the killings won't stop. And if he's already fired when the next one happens, where does that leave us? Where does that leave you, the program, the university, this whole fucking town?"

Reggie didn't go home. She went to her office, left the lights off and locked the door behind her. She sat for quite a while in the dark, thinking. About Denny. She could not put together the Denny who had pledged infinite patience last night, with the one who looked very much capable of bashing hers and Jonathan Manx's skulls in tonight. And she wondered -- as she was sure Denny believed -- if tonight had ended it between them. How could either of them get past what had happened in Manx's office this night?

"Everybody has demons," Ann Bonano had told her. But it was hard enough living with your own let alone trying to live with someone else's demons.

As frightening as the experience had been, if she stood back from it far enough, she couldn't really blame Denny. This had obviously been a move bred out of desperation. He'd come to Diamond Cove on the promise of a quiet little town, far removed from the daily tragedies and horrors he'd witnessed on the streets of Chicago. And now? Four murders -- five deaths if you counted the fallout of Andy Broder's suicide -- in less than a week.

She agreed with Denny's gut feeling that there must be some tie between the two Danning murders and the Broder killings because Karen Danning and Andy Broder had both been treated at the university, even though Karen hadn't gone through Jonathan Manx's "inner child" sessions, and the boy hadn't had what

Manx liked to think of as a "breakthrough." But then there was Frank Cole's caveat that there was no link between the two families.

Reggie switched on her desk lamp, rummaged around in her desk for some index cards and thumb tacks. On one card she wrote KAREN DANNING and tacked it to the corkboard mounted on the wall over her desk. A little below it she affixed a second card: ALAN DANNING. On the other side of the board, another card: BRODERS. A little below that one: ANDY BRODER.

Frank Cole was right; there was no connection…*between the families.*

But there was a nexus where they all came together.

Chapter Ten

Reggie turned on to 495 South, and the highway wound a quiet way through central Massachusetts, Diamond Cove falling farther and farther behind. With each mile, she felt a certain internal easing. She hadn't realized how tightly wound she'd become over the last few days until all the reasons for it -- the killings, and yes, Denny Petit -- were miles behind her.

She'd been up since six, early enough, she thought, to avoid bumping into Ann Bonano and having to explain herself. She left a note shoved under Ann's door asking her to keep an eye on her apartment, that she'd be back in a few days. She had called Jonathan Manx's office, knowing he wouldn't be in for hours, leaving a voicemail message that she had been called away on a personal emergency but would be returning soon.

Then she climbed in her car, turned her cell phone off, and headed out.

There were two routes south she could take. The more direct one was to hop on Interstate 95, roughly paralleling the coast, taking her straight through first Boston, then later, New York City, and then finally onto the New Jersey Turnpike which would take her to her final destination. Instead, she opted to jump off 95 for 495 soon after crossing the Massachusetts border; the first leg of a route cutting on a diagonal across Massachusetts, Connecticut, avoiding New York City by taking her west across the Tappan Zee Bridge, and then south to pick up the northern end of New Jersey's Garden State Parkway.

It was a longer route, but she justified it telling herself there was a lot less trucking, the traffic was lighter for most of the run, and it was a generally prettier drive.

All of which she knew, at some deep level, had nothing to do with her choice.

She had not set out with it in mind to see her father; that could only be a distraction from her real purpose. But then she'd realized the southwestern route would bring her more or less in his vicinity, and then it had finally sunk in that she was going to see him; that she *needed* to see him, and maybe, that, too, was a real purpose.

It had nothing to do with Denny, it had everything to do with Denny. Maybe they were through; they'd certainly hit some cataclysmic bumps in the last few days, hell, in the last few hours. But that wasn't going to put her demons to rest, and if she had learned one thing from her years of practice, the first step in dealing with demons was identifying them. You can't fight what you can't face.

The prettiest thing about Belleville was its name and the prettiness ended there. The town was part of that great, unbroken urban sprawl radiating out from nearby Newark. When her father had been young, it had been a blue-collar, working-class town, heavily Italian, where families were raised on decent paychecks earned at local factories. But the factories were all gone, the Italian families that hadn't died out had moved to the suburbs, and the town was now composed of worn-looking enclaves of Blacks, Hispanics, Filipinos, Indians, Pakistanis, most struggling at the kind of jobs that weren't going to pay *their* way out to the suburbs.

Her father still lived in the same house she'd been raised in; a non-descript, boxy two-story affair on a street of non-descript, boxy two-story affairs, all with the same tired look, same small square of patchy lawn, same cracked walk.

Reggie pulled up to the curb in front of the house. Her father was home; his Cadillac Sedan de Ville (good God, he still had that thing?) was in the driveway. She remembered when he'd brought it home; his first new car, and by God, it was a Cadillac! She also remembered that, even then, she could pick up on where her father's attentions were focused, thinking he showed more love for that goddamned car than for anybody in the family.

She sat for a while, looking at her father's car and her father's house. Her own car was still idling; she had only to slip it into "Drive" and get back on the Parkway.

Which, she told herself, would've been the chickenshit way to go.

She killed the engine, took a breath, and climbed out of the car. She took another breath and started up the walk.

She was only halfway to the door when it swung open and there was Donny McLaren. He still had the broad shoulders and massive hands that had lugged and piled lumber and cinderblocks when he'd started working as a laborer decades ago, but his middle was now as thick as his shoulders. The thick, wavy red hair had thinned and grown speckled with white, the wide flat face had gone soft and jowly, his eyes now seemed lost inside puffs of flesh. He wore a frayed sweater over a T-shirt, faded work twills he hadn't retired when he had, and slippers.

Reggie stood on the walk while he stared at her, his face showing nothing. Then he gave a strange sort of huff and sighed out a slow, "Damn..."

"Do I get to come in?"

He said nothing but stepped back and out of the way. Reggie walked past, careful not to look him in the eye; to not give him the satisfaction of acknowledging him.

He'd kept the house clean -- he'd always been something of a martinet about how the house needed to be maintained -- but it was as worn inside as the outside; the furniture was the same furniture she'd remembered growing up with, blankets now covering the worn fabric of the sofa and chairs, the wall paint now drab and faded.

"G'ahead 'n' sit," her father said, closing the door, nodding her to the sofa.

He took a seat on a cushioned chair across the room from her, grabbed the remote off the scuffed coffee table in front of him to turn off whatever sports event he'd been watching. She smiled ruefully at that; there'd always been some kind of damned game for him to watch, alone, demanding not to be interrupted except to be brought food and drink, like some medieval king. "How long's it been, Junior?"

"I always hated when you called me that. It's Regina, Dad. Did you forget?"

"I didn't forget…Regina."

"Last time would've been Mom's funeral."

"How long before that?"

"Long enough I don't remember," and she made sure to sound glad she didn't remember.

"When you went off to college. To make yourself smart. Did it work?"

It was hard not to smile. "I'm not sure."

"You gonna come to *my* funeral?"

"Why? You planning on one soon?"

He made a wry face. "Don't be so eager. Only the good die young."

"Then you'll probably outlive me. But in case you don't, I'll be there…to piss on your grave."

He smiled. "Nice to see you're mellowing. It's nice that you'd come. I'll have it in my will they have to have toilet paper at the graveside. Drink? Coffee?"

"Nothing."

"Of course. You mind if I…?"

She nodded for him to go ahead. He disappeared into the back of the house, the kitchen. She heard the refrigerator open and close, the pop-hiss of him opening a can of beer, then he was back. He held up the can in toast to her, took a sip, sat back in his chair. "Well, I know you're not here 'cause you're homesick or 'cause you miss your good ol' pop."

"I have business down south; this was on the way."

He nodded although she could tell he didn't completely believe her. "You're not gonna believe this; I'm glad you stopped by. I don't see many people since I retired."

"Well, you were never big on making friends."

He surprised her by not getting angry over the barb. He had always bristled at the least, littlest bit of criticism, more so when it was on target. Instead, his face grew soft. He stared into the open top of his beer. "No. No, I wasn't." He looked up at her. "So, why'd you come by…Regina?"

"I have a question."

"Shoot."

"Why were you such a miserable shit to mom?"

"Oh." He lay back in his chair, as if some great suspense had been resolved.

"I get why you hated me --"

His puffy eyes opened wide. "You thought I hated you?"

"You hated I wasn't a son."

"Not the same thing."

She waved that away. "I'm not going to argue semantics with you. Why'd you hate mom so much?"

That same pensive look down into his beer. "I didn't hate her, Junior, um, Regina."

"Jesus, you didn't act like you loved her! You didn't act like you even *liked* her!"

He nodded; he understood. "Well, here's something else you won't believe. Been a few years she's gone, I've been thinking 'bout that all this time. Why I couldn'ta been nicer."

"And what'd you come up with?"

"I think…" He smiled, oddly, knowing he wouldn't be believed, that it would be taken as ridiculous. "I think I was afraid."

Reggie almost laughed. "Afraid? Of what? Afraid of *mom?*"

He took a deep pull on his beer, set it down on the coffee table, pulled himself to his feet. He buried his hands in his pockets and stood at the front windows, looking out at the street he'd been watching die bit by bit for decades. He took a deep breath, let it out in a sigh. "You didn't know your grandfather. I mean my father, Grandpa Ian. You woulda liked him. He was nice like you probably like 'em. But his wife, your grandma, Maeve, she was a bitch on wheels, and don't go gettin' all Me Too on me, that's what she was. She broke that man, my dad, I watched her break him into a million pieces. I always believed -- still do -- that's what killed him so early. Forty-two and he dies of a heart attack. She killed his heart, your grandma."

"So, you swore that was never going to happen to you, that when you got married, you'd pick a woman *you* could bully and push around."

He hung his head. Was that…shame? "Sorta, I guess. Like I said, I've had a lot of time to myself to run it 'round in my head, and I think there was somethin' else." He turned back to her, and Reggie could see it in his face: Please understand. "Your mom was nice, and she was sweet…like my dad. It drove me nuts as a kid that he didn't fight back."

"So, you hated that in mom, but when she did push back --"

"'Cause *that* was Grandma Maeve!" He shook his head, realizing there was no way to make it make sense. He went back to his chair, dropped tiredly into it. "You want me to say I was a shitty husband?"

"And a shitty dad."

"And a shitty dad? I was. Even when I was acting bad to her, part of me would say, stop, knock it off, what the hell's a matter with you, Donny? But I couldn't stop. You're the shrink; you tell me why. You gonna sit there and tell me there's never a time when your head is tellin' you to go right and you still go left?"

Sure, Reggie thought, that's how I ended up *here!* She stood and headed for the door.

"Where you goin'?" as he grunted to his feet.

"I told you; I have business, I've got to get back on the road." She was hurrying now, had the door open. She didn't want to hear any more because it was coming to her, she wasn't going to hear what she needed to hear.

"I know what you want!" and now he sounded defiant, calling to her from the doorway as she hurried down the walk. "Look, I know I didn't treat you two right, but no use sayin' I'm sorry now. I can't take any of it back. There's too much done and it's too late for, 'I'm sorry.'"

She was standing in her open car door now. "Maybe, Dad. But 'I'm sorry' would've been a nice start." She started to slide into her car but stopped. "You want my professional opinion on why you couldn't change?"

He nodded but she could tell he wasn't expecting anything good. She made sure not to disappoint him: "Because some people are just assholes."

Reggie's GPS took her from the main offices of Philadelphia's Behavioral Health Division through a maze of narrow, busy streets, all of which seemed to be one-way and always a one-way she didn't want to go. Eventually, she found the community health center she'd been looking for; a converted pre-war row house, its front gayly painted in graffiti style with images of the kind of happy urban residents who would never need the center's services.

Inside, she was pointed to the director's office on the third floor ("No elevator, sorry!" and Reggie was glad for the stamina and strong legs she'd built up from her daily jogs) where she was told the director would be with her as soon as he could.

There had been times back in New York when Reggie had had to deal with city services, and looking around the cramped, cluttered office, the desk submerged in folders and paperwork pushed aside to barely make room for an unfinished lunch of fast food, it occurred to her, sadly, they all looked the same: overwhelmed. And so, too, did the people who worked there.

She heard a loud yet tired voice from out in the hall: "I *know*, Louise, I already called, I called him four times and I'm *still* waiting to hear! Don't worry; one way or another, I'll take care of it. I know, I told you I'll take care of it! *I'll take care of it, Louise!*"

And then Dr. Elliott Schaefer appeared in the doorway: middle-aged but a worn middle-aged, with a fleshy, sagging face, reading glasses parked on his bald pate, his baggy suit pants, pushed down by the bulge of his fast food-fed belly, clashing with battered tennis shoes. He was holding a toilet plunger. At the sight of Reggie, he pulled his sagging self to attention, held up the plunger and made a sign of the cross: "Ye are welcome, stranger!" he announced, then sighed tiredly, tossed the plunger carelessly into a corner and crossed the small office with the flat-footed trudge of someone who was permanently exhausted.

"Now," he said, dropping heavily into his chair, "do I know you? Am I supposed to know you? Did I know you were going to be here?"

Reggie smiled. "Dr. McLaren. At the division offices, they told me they'd call ahead to let you know I was coming."

Schaefer ran a wide, hairy-backed hand across his rubbery face, as if trying to wake himself up. "They probably did, but if it was more than five minutes ago, I'll be damned if I remember."

"It was more than five minutes ago."

"Ah, well then, there ya go! I'm sorry; you're catching me at the end of the day, and I've spent the last twenty minutes in a fight-to-the-death with the downstairs toilet. I think the plumbing in this place hasn't been upgraded since they built the building back around the, oh, I'd guess the Stone Age." Schaefer looked unhappily at the French fries on his desk which had clotted into a single, cold, tangled mass. With a resigned sigh, he pulled a few of them apart and started munching. "Sorry, again, for eating in front of you, but I didn't get to finish my lunch. The way things are going, this looks like it's going to be dinner, too. Maybe tomorrow's breakfast. So, Dr. McLaren, who looks too well-dressed and rested to work for the city, what can I do you for?"

"I was told Frank Cole worked for you."

Schaefer brightened. "Frankie? Oh, yeah! Do you know him?"

"We're on the faculty together at Diamond Cove."

"I'm glad he got the gig! I wrote his letter of recommendation, ya know. How's he doing up there?"

"The semester hasn't started yet, so…"

"I hope it works out for him. I'd been pushing him to find something else for a while. I was the one who saw the job posting, practically had to twist his arm to get him to put in for it."

"Why? Was there a problem here? Was he not good at his job?"

Schaefer smiled sadly. "Problem was he was *too* good at his job."

Reggie shook her head, not understanding.

Schaefer took a bite of his half-eaten cold cheeseburger. "Tell me this isn't the picture of desperation. Not like this in the private sector, is it?"

"Not very no," Reggie said a little guiltily. "You were saying about Frank being *too* good at his job?"

Schaefer threw the burger down onto its wrapper, took a sip from what Reggie was sure was a warm soda diluted with melted ice, and made a sour face. "It works a little differently around here than I'm sure it worked with your practice. We don't get to choose patients, we don't get to say, hey, we're full up, try another shrink. And nobody comes to us because they've got some mild neurosis about, like, I dunno; what's a good mild urban uptown neurosis?"

"I get the picture."

"Thing is, you do this a few years, you've got three ways to go: you do a kind of mental triage, helping the ones you think you can help, and then you blow by the cases you know you can't. And, man, there's a lot you can't. You get some twelve-year-old in here and he's already so damaged by his shitty home life -- forgive my language -- you know you've already got a child sociopath on your hands, and nothing you do is going to keep him from spending his life in and out of jail. So, you say, Ok, I'm done, and move on to the next case.

"Or you go nuts yourself.

"Or you spend every night crying in your beer."

He thought for a moment. "Maybe there's a fourth; you spend every night crying in your beer *until* you go nuts. Or maybe it's the other way around."

"I'm guessing Frank couldn't take the triage route."

"God bless that guy, he bled for every one of his cases." Schaefer pointed at some bound volumes on the windowsill he was using as a bookshelf. "I've got studies there -- you've probably seen them -- on what the burnout rate is for people who do this job: anywhere from twenty-one-percent to two-thirds wind up fried. They get cynical, they stop caring, they push clients through like they're on the checkout line at the supermarket. And, yeah, me, too; I'm no exception. If I'd had half a brain, I wouldn't've told Frankie about that job up in Maine; *I* should've gone after it!"

"Why didn't you?"

Schaefer looked around his office, too little space for too much paper. "Beats hell outta me, Doctor."

"But not Frank?"

"I don't know how he kept at it." He nodded over a thought. "Of course, I think about it and I get it."

"What do you mean?" Reggie asked.

"Empathy."

She still didn't understand.

"He never told you?"

"About what?"

"His family." He hesitated. "I don't know why I'm being shy. It's public record. When Frank was a kid, his mom was murdered. That's not the worst of it. They think the perp was his *dad*. I don't know the details, but I don't think they ever caught the guy. That's as much as Frank ever told me, and you can understand me not feeling comfortable trying to get more out of him about it."

Reggie felt a cold bolt run through her body. "Do you, um, know…*how* she was killed?"

"Like I said, I didn't ask. He only ever talked about it once. Came up over one of his cases, a domestic abuse number. Ya know, I didn't think to ask you; what's this all about?"

Reggie had her story prepared: "Nothing, really. As I said, we're working together now, I happened to be in the neighborhood, thought I'd try to find out a little bit about the guy, maybe get some idea of the best way to work with him, see what his strengths are, so forth."

Schaefer's head cocked to one side; he didn't quite buy it but was willing to roll with it. "Frankie's easy. He's committed; the guy really cares. Maybe too much, like I said, but I liked having him here. There's, um, not a problem with him, is there?"

Reggie shook her head. "I guess I was just nosy."

Schaefer didn't seem to completely buy that, either. "Anything else I can do for you?" But generosity wasn't behind it; she could tell that now he was looking after Cole and trying to ease her out of his office.

She nodded, her way of saying, I get it, and started for the door.

"Dr. McLaren?"

She stopped, halfway into the hall.

Schaefer gave her a doubtful face. "I don't know what this is *really* about, but Frank Cole was not only one of the nicest guys I've ever worked with, but one of the best clinicians I ever had working under me. I can't say it enough; the guy really *cares!*"

"Of that, Dr. Schaefer, I have no doubt." That, Reggie said to herself, may be the problem.

Reggie battled her way through rush hour traffic and across the Benjamin Franklin Bridge back into New Jersey. The highway on the Jersey side was lined with hotels and motels. She pulled into the first decent one she saw, took a room, ordered up a salad from room service, changed into her sweats, propped herself up against the head of the bed with her laptop parked on her thighs.

She was prowling around the Internet for a good hour before she finally pulled up a story from the archives of one of the Philadelphia daily papers dated 27 years earlier. The headline read:

6-YEAR-OLD WITNESSES MOM'S MURDER. COPS SUSPECT MISSING DAD

And below that:

Darryla Cole, 29, life-long resident of the Fishtown area, was found beaten to death in her home yesterday. Suspected in the killing is her husband, Robert Cole, 30, a metalworker. According to police, the only witness to the crime was Francis Cole, the couple's 6-year-old son, currently being treated for shock at Kensington Hospital.

As Reggie read on, apparently there'd been a years-long history of police making disturbing the peace and domestic violence calls to the household, including two arrests (charges dropped when Darryla refused to press charges). Neighbors had complained for years of constant fights between the couple.

"My heart always broke for the little boy," one neighbor was quoted as saying. "I thought it was bad enough that he had to see his dad treating his mom so bad all the time, but then this? It kills you to think of him living with this."

As for Robert Cole, the police had issued an APB but had no leads on his whereabouts.

Reggie continued searching Philadelphia news sites, but there were no follow-up stories. Darryla Cole's murder was one of the city's four hundred-odd homicides that year, and as such, just another all-too-typical big city tragedy soon forgotten in the never-ending flow of big city tragedies.

On a hunch, Reggie began a wider search, looking outside the Pennsylvania/New Jersey area for any mention of Francis Cole or his father. After another hour of Internet-crawling, she came across a small story in a Milwaukee newspaper:

MURDERED MAN LINKED TO OLD PHILADELPHIA KILLING

According to the story, Robert Cole had been living under an assumed name in Milwaukee for several years, working at a local sheet metal plant. When he didn't show up for work three days in a row, a friend of his from work stopped by Cole's apartment to check up on him. He found Cole's apartment door unlocked and Cole laying on the living room floor, beaten to death with a ball peen hammer found in his kitchen sink. When police figured out that Cole's identification was fake, they ran a fingerprint check and that kicked out his real identity and the tie to the still-open murder case in Philadelphia.

According to the Milwaukee police, Cole's neighbors and co-workers said he had pretty much kept to himself. There were no leads on a perpetrator.

There was no mention of Frank Cole.

Reggie looked at the date of the story and did some math. Frank Cole's father's death would've occurred the summer after Frank had graduated college.

Chapter Eleven

One thing Reggie had come to love about Maine, even in her short time there, was the sunsets. By the time she was turning up Denny Petit's rutted drive, the sky in the west had turned a brilliant orange-gold, graduating across the sky into shades of velvety purple, set behind a lacy frame of treetops. She pulled to a stop next to Denny's SUV, killed the engine…and then just sat.

Part of it was simple fatigue; she'd logged a lot of highway miles in the last 38 hours. But the other part…

She'd spent the ride back up from south Jersey wondering what to say to Denny, how to say it…and what not to say. The personal and the professional had become so intertwined that even now, after hours on the road trying to work it out in her head, she still wasn't clear on what she would say or do, and might've sat there all night except…

"Are you alright?"

She looked up in the mirror and saw Denny standing in the wedge of warm, yellow light spilling out of the open front door of his trailer.

Well, Chickenshit, she said to herself, time to do this…

She took a deep breath and hauled herself stiffly, tiredly out of her car.

He took a step toward her, then stopped himself, shoved his hands deep in his pockets as if afraid of what they might do if left loose. Softly, then: "Are you ok, Reggie?"

She shook her head, confused, not sure how to answer. She stayed by her car.

After a moment, after he had waited but she said nothing, "I thought I wouldn't get to see you again." He looked down, embarrassed. "I was *afraid* I wouldn't see you again. You know; after the other night in Manx's office." Then, almost mumbling, "I've missed you."

She smiled. "What happened to patience?"

He smiled in return. "Doesn't mean I wouldn't miss seeing you." Then the smile faded. "I thought maybe after that night…I was afraid maybe that spooked you into leaving town."

"You knew I was gone?"

Denny turned away, shaking his head at his own conduct. "It's embarrassing; I've been like some…some kind of *kid*. I drove by the school. I drove by the house where you live. Just hoping I'd, you know…see you." He looked up at the darkening sky, shaking his head, again. "Stupid, stupid. Juvenile."

"And if you had seen me?"

He turned back to her. "I would've kept going. I made a promise. But like I said, I missed you. I'm not a stalker, it's not like that. This is embarrassing, acting like this. Oh, shit," and he turned away once more, "I can feel myself blushing, for Christ's sake. What am I, thirteen?"

It was hard for Reggie not to laugh silently. "I've been practicing therapy long enough to know that the only difference between boys and men is men can shave. That, and maybe they're under the delusion they know what they're doing in any given situation."

Denny nodded emphatically in agreement. "Well, I won't argue with that." He took a step toward her, and for a second, Reggie considered taking a step back…but she didn't.

"I have to ask, Reg." She could see him steeling himself for bad news. "I…I almost don't want to, but I have to; did that night finish us?"

And now she walked toward him. She pulled his right hand from his pocket, held it softly between both of hers. "We have a lot to talk about, Denny. And it's not all about you. And we'll have that talk. But this isn't the time. That's not why I'm here."

He cocked his head, puzzled.

"Can I come inside?"

He led her by the hand into his trailer. He quickly moved to turn off the TV, gestured her to a chair. She nodded it away and asked for a pen and paper. She followed him into the cramped kitchen where a small memo pad with attached pencil was held to the refrigerator with a magnet. She set the pad on the crowded counter and drew a diagram similar to what she had tacked to her corkboard the night before last: the names of Karen, Marcia, David, and Alan Danning down one side of the paper, Andy Broder, and his parents down the other.

"When Karen Danning was killed, we were looking at Marcia as a possible perp, maybe even her son," she said. "But then the Broders were killed, and none of the Dannings knew them, so that junked that theory. But then Alan Danning went down, and we started looking at Marcia and David, again…and then…" She felt her face flush.

"And then?"

"Um…"

Denny sighed. "And then it was hard not to remember that time I roughed up Alan."

She pushed quickly past that: "But that wouldn't explain the Broders. You didn't know them. So, no connection between the families. Then you thought because Karen and Andy Broder had been treated at the university, maybe Jonathan had turned them into --. What did you call them?"

"Little Frankensteins, I believe."

"Except Karen hadn't gone through that program, and Andy never completed it."

"So, Jonathan says."

"So, he says, but let's go with that for the moment; that they didn't go through that program…but they were both receiving treatment through the school." She drew a line from Karen Danning to the middle of the paper, from Marcia Danning to the same spot, another line from Andy Broder to the middle of the paper, leaving just enough space between the three lines to write:

FRANK

COLE

"He's the connection," Reggie said. "They all intersect at him. He treated all three of them."

Denny stepped back, shaking his head violently as he walked in small circles -- all the little kitchen would allow -- his hands up as if surrendering. "Wait, wait, wait, that still doesn't make any sense!"

"I'm afraid it does. Has Frank ever talked to you…about his past?"

Denny had stopped all his moving about, leaned against the refrigerator. Reggie could see that Denny Petit, the good cop, was now working the facts mentally; critically, analytically. "Yeah, about his work in Philly. So?"

"Further back."

"How far?"

Reggie told him what she'd found out about the murder of Frank Cole's mother, about Cole having witnessed the brutal killing, and about Cole's father turning up similarly murdered sixteen years later.

Denny sagged, his head shaking, connecting the dots but not wanting to see the final picture. "I…I can't…I *can't*…"

"You don't *want* to believe it. Neither do I, Denny."

Denny straightened up; the doubt gone. "I need to look at his patient files, Reggie." Firm.

She nodded but walked away, into the living room, dropped heavily onto the sofa where she'd been sipping wine with Denny -- … Good, God, was that just a few nights ago?

"I know," she said. "But if I help you do that, I'm told it could result in 'a probable suspension and possible loss of position.' That's a quote if you didn't pick up on it."

Denny sat in his chair across the small room. Reggie smiled a little; on the TV table where there'd been pizza the other night was now a take-out container from The Clipper.

"You can come with me to the building," she said, "because you want to visit with me, spend some time exchanging pleasantries with a friend. Then, because of your overactive bladder, you excuse yourself, and with your fifteen dollars' worth of hardware, gain entry to Frank's office and files. Then you come back and say to me -- me, who doesn't know that you've undertaken said break-in -- and say, Hey, I just learned some interesting things about some person or persons whose names I won't tell you, this is just some hypotheticals; can you explain to me in layman's terms what might be going on with them?"

Denny laughed, but then grew serious: "Does that cover you."

She shrugged. "Maybe. Barely. If that. But it's no cover at all for you."

Denny laughed, again. It occurred to Reggie she hadn't seen Denny laugh nearly enough, and she would like to see it more. "My dear, after this is wrapped up, I'm not sure I even want to be a meter maid let alone a cop."

"Hey, Reg!"

Reggie stirred. She'd been sitting at her desk, and the accumulated miles of the last two long days had been catching up to her; her eyes had started to slide closed.

"Reggie!"

It was Denny, from down the hall in Frank Cole's office. Reggie pulled herself out of her chair, yawned, pinched her cheeks so she could look -- and feel -- at least semi-conscious, then shuffled down the dark corridor to the open door of Cole's office.

Denny was sitting cross-legged on the floor by the short file cabinet by Cole's desk he'd managed to jimmy open. He had several manila folders open and spread out on the floor in front of him. "You should hear this," and he nodded her toward the desk chair.

Reggie nodded for him to go ahead, afraid that if she sat, she'd start to doze again.

"'Broder, Andrew,'" Denny read, "'It is a prescription for adolescent psychological disaster; an emotionally abusive father enabled by a weak mother who has long since retreated into the background of her son's upbringing. The situation may already be beyond remediation. At this point, the only possible salvation for the subject is the removal of the most damaging element in that dynamic'." Denny looked up at Reggie. "'Removal of the most damaging element'. Frank keeps diligent notes; every entry is dated. According to his notation, the Broders were killed the night of the day he wrote this."

Denny tossed the folder aside, picked up another one. "Karen Danning," he said, then flipped through looking for a specific spot. He began reading, following his fingertip as it skipped from one salient point to the next: "Let's see, um, yeah, here: '...despite her obvious regret for the emotional damage done to her daughter...still maintains a certain level of denial about her own culpability...apparently oblivious to the manipulations of her husband and the possibility of continuing to damage her daughter emotionally through her attempts to reconnect through her grandson at the urging of her husband...'"

Reggie had a cold, sinking feeling in her stomach. "Let me guess. The day Karen Danning was killed."

Denny nodded and tossed the folder aside. "You told me Frank had only treated Karen and Marcia Danning and the Broder kid."

"As far as I know."

"But he's got files here on the whole circus: all the Dannings, even Marcia's kid, David, that Broder kid's parents -- ..." With each name he had pointed to one of the folders in front of him, but had stopped himself, his finger hovering over one unnamed file. The finger folded back into his fist.

Now Reggie sat. It wasn't fatigue. As the evidence mounted, her legs began to feel wobbly under her. "Christ, he wasn't treating them," she said. "He was observing them, diagnosing them...*indicting* them..." She sank into the chair with a sigh. "Condemning them."

Denny nodded in grim agreement. He picked up another folder. "Marcia Danning. 'It is clear that Marcia has militantly applied herself to protect both her and her son from any further emotional damage, but as a result of the psychological scarring suffered from the predations of her stepfather and the negligence of her mother, Marcia's protective stance presents less as the ministrations of a loving mother and more like the oppressive, dictatorial conduct of any resented authoritarian figure. The tragic paradox is that Marcia, in trying to shield her son, is undoubtedly doing more emotional harm to him than good. The speculation that she might relax her domineering behavior once the major offending element had been removed has since proven wrong…'"

"'Major offending element.' Alan Danning."

Denny nodded. "Reggie… This note about Marcia is dated *today*. Karen Danning, Alan Danning, the Broders; they all had some kind of note like this the day they were killed. The clock's running on that girl."

"What're you going to do?"

Denny dropped the last folder, leaned forward, and put his head in his hands. "I have to take him in."

"Denny, you can't! A first-year law school student could pop him free before you could turn the key on the lock." She waved at the folders spread out on the floor. "I've dealt with enough police officers to know none of this constitutes evidence. Even if you could get it admitted -- which, since it was obtained illegally, you can't -- it doesn't prove anything. All you've got in those files is him saying some people are shitty parents! You had no probable cause for breaking in --"

Denny held up a halting hand. "Hey, Miss ACLU, I get it! What am I supposed to do? Wait for him to pop his cork again and run his score up to five?"

Reggie thought for a moment. "Maybe a psychiatric hold. These files don't enter into it. I say what I found out in Philly gave me some reason to think maybe Frank's cracking under the strain; in my professional opinion I think he might be a danger to himself… That might be enough to get a 24-hour hold."

"Jesus, Reg, that's thinner than your story to get us in here."

She shrugged. "It buys us some time."

"Time to…?"

"To see if we can find something more concrete."

Denny started gathering up the files into a single stack, hesitating when he reached for the one file to which he hadn't given a name. He gave Reggie a glance, one she couldn't decipher, looking as if he were about to say something, then changed his mind, added the file to the stack and dropped them back into Cole's file cabinet. "I'll lock up," he said and waved her out.

She waited for him back at her office, heard him and his hardware rattling around with Cole's office door, then he was in her doorway. He looked…not so much tired as sapped, propped against the doorsill. "I'm going to have one of my people go over to Marcia Danning's place with an order to detain if Frank shows up."

"And you?"

Denny looked pained. "I don't disbelieve you, Reg, about Frank. It's -- … I mean, even this stuff about, what was it? Compartmenting --"

"Compartmentalizing."

"This is still hard to get my head around. This is Frank Cole! He was --. He *is* my friend! He's done me a lot of good. I owe it to him…to be the one. I'll go for him."

"I should go with you."

"You?"

"I might be able to help you talk to him. Why not?"

He took a long, disturbing moment. "Was…Was Frank…Did he ever treat you?"

"You mean professionally? No. We talked some, but -- …" Then she caught the look on Denny's face, and she felt a chill. "Why?"

"He had a file on you."

"Me?"

"I can't quote it exactly, but stuff to the effect that he figured you had your own emotional scars growing up, and that's why -- …" Denny looked away.

"Why *what?"*

"Why you were hurting me. His words, Reggie, not mine."

But like so much of what Frank Cole had noted in his observations, it wasn't untrue, and Reggie felt her cheeks grow hot.

"I'm sorry, Denny."

"I said they were his words, Reggie. I'm not saying it."

"But --"

"I'm not saying it."

She nodded and let it go at that.

"I think he was the one who tore up your dolls," Denny said. "I think it was a good thing you went to Philadelphia when you did."

"Why?"

"Because that entry was dated yesterday. I want you to stay here, lock yourself in. I'm going to send somebody over here to keep an eye on you until I have Frank in custody. I figure you're as much a target right now as Marcia Danning. Come lock the door after I leave."

She followed him to the front doors of the building. She stopped him as he reached for the door.

"Denny, I don't know how he'll react when he's confronted with this. Especially by someone he considers a friend. He could look at that as a betrayal. You should bring somebody with you as a back-up. What I'm saying is -- …"

He waited for the rest. "Be careful?" he offered.

But what she wanted to say was stuck in her throat, and her cheeks flushed, again, but for a different reason then Frank Cole's cut-to-the-bone diagnosis. Or maybe that was, after all, a part of it.

Chickenshit. Well, if the words wouldn't come…

She reached up, slipped an arm around Denny's neck, and pulled her face close to his, pressed her lips against his, and fought the urge to scream, don't go! Send someone else!

She hadn't realized how hard she was holding on to him until she felt him pulling her arm away. Even in the dark corridor, with only the glare from the streetlights outside, she could see him smiling. Then he gently pushed her away and reached for the door.

"Lock this after me."

She let the door swing closed behind him, Denny disappearing behind the white glare on the door glass.

"Be careful," she said, and it sounded oh so small in the dark, empty lobby.

Chapter Twelve

Reggie was halfway back to her office when she froze with a thought. She went back to the front doors, looked across the quad and saw the lights in the library were still on. She looked at her watch: nearly seven, they'd be closing soon. She unlocked the door and started trotting across the quad.

She had thought about going back to her office for her phone to tell Denny that Marcia Danning might not be home, she might be at her job at the library. But then Reggie thought to let it go; Denny was sending a man to watch Marcia's apartment house, and that was still not a bad idea -- keep all the bases covered. She also knew Denny only had three men at his disposal. He was already sending one to babysit her on campus, and hopefully he had taken her advice and was taking another with him to Frank Cole's. If Marcia were at the library, Reggie could bring her back to her office and wait for Denny's assigned babysitter with her.

Reggie got to the library doors just as one of the full-timers, a middle-aged matronly type, was just coming to the door, pocketbook in hand, coat over her arm, obviously leaving for the night.

"I was just ready to lock up," the woman said.

"Is Marcia Danning on tonight?"

"Why, yes, but we're closing –"

"I'm faculty, Marcia is one of my students and it's really, really important I talk to her. It's about a special project she's supposed to do for me."

"What's your name?"

Reggie told her, the woman motioned her to wait at the door, went back to the check-out desk, picked up a phone. A moment later, she was back. "I can't say she was happy to hear it was you."

"Students are never happy to hear from their instructors," Reggie said, and the woman smiled and nodded.

"Don't take too long," the woman said. "She's up on the fourth floor putting books back on the shelves. I know she'd like to finish up and get home. She has a son, you know."

"I know."

The woman let Reggie pass and Reggie heard her lock the front doors behind her. There was an elevator off the lobby, and she took it to the fourth floor.

It took a minute or so to locate Marcia among the maze of bookstacks, walking up and down one aisle as she found the proper places for the books on a cart she'd parked nearby. She showed no sign she'd heard Reggie, never looked away from what she was doing. "You're not my teacher, there is no special project, and we don't even like each other. Well, *I* don't like *you*. I only said yes to letting you up here because I was curious why you'd fling so much bullshit to see me." Then she did finally stop what she was doing and fixed Reggie with hard eyes and a mean smile. "But now, seeing you face-to-face, I realize I don't care that much." She turned back to her books. "G'bye."

"You need to come with me, Marcia. Now!"

Marcia chuckled. "Actually, lady, I don't have to do shit with you so --"

"There's a police car already on its way to your place and another one on the way here. You have --"

And now Marcia was alarmed. "Cops? My place? Is David ok?"

"He should be."

"What the hell does *that* mean? 'Should be'?"

"Marcia, we may not have much time --"

"*Make* time! What do you mean: 'should be'? What's going on with my son?"

"He's not after David."

The emotions were all crashing together on Marcia Danning's face; fear for her son, confusion, and out of the mix of the two, anger. "Who's not -- … What the *fuck* are you talking about?"

Reggie realized she wasn't making much sense. She had not wanted to panic Marica, but now saw the best route was the direct one. "We --. The police, the chief; he knows who the killer is. You're on his list. Maybe tonight."

Marcia froze, blinking as if some bright flash had gone off in front of her face as she tried to digest it all.

"You need to come with me," Reggie said, slowly walking toward Marcia, reaching out to her. "There's a policeman on his way to my office. We can both wait –"

The lights went out.

Reggie felt her way back along the stacks to the main aisle where there was a feeble light through the windows from the moon, spill from streetlights outside. Don't panic, she told herself. Not yet.

Then Marcia was standing alongside her. "That's just Mrs. Dickinson," she said. "She was going to lock up. She turns off the lights --"

"If she's that motherly type I passed on my way in, she left five minutes ago." Ok, Reggie told herself, you can panic now. But then she could hear her father's voice; I didn't teach you to panic when the pressure's on, Junior. "Do you have your cell phone with you?"

"In my pocketbook down at the front desk. You?"

"Left it in my office." Keep it together, she kept telling herself. This is *definitely* not the time to go chickenshit. I know right now you want to curl up in a ball on the floor, but you *both* need to *keep it together!* She took Marcia by the hand and pulled her to the elevator, but the buttons refused to light up when she stabbed at them.

"It's not just the lights," Marcia said. "Power's off."

Reggie pointed to the wall phone by the elevator.

"Internal only," Marcia said, answering the unasked question. "The only lines to the outside are the phones at the front desk."

Footsteps -- a slow trudge -- echoed up the stairwell.

"Any other stairs?" Reggie fought to keep the strain out of her voice.

"Just the fire stairs. But an alarm goes off when they open. Hit the door, and he'll know which stairwell we're in."

Reggie gauged the footsteps coming up from the stairwell were now just two floors below them.

There may not have been much light on the floor, but it was enough for Reggie to see Marcia's face. If the woman was afraid, it was somewhere buried under cold determination. If there was one positive that had come out of her nightmarish life in the Danning household, it was this: she was a fighter. You would've loved this one, Dad, she said to herself.

Ok, then, Reggie told herself, then we *both* fight. No more chickenshits here. "C'mon," and she pulled Marcia along with her toward the nearest fire stairs.

Marcia pulled back. "I told you --"

"I know," Reggie said and kept tugging at Marcia who finally let herself get pulled along.

Mounted on the wall near the fire stairs was a fire alarm. Reggie punched through the glass cover with her elbow and pulled the alarm tab, then pulled Marcia through the fire door after her, the door alarm joining the clanging main alarm ripping apart the quiet of the library, the darkness broken by the bright white flashes of the emergency lights mounted on the walls.

In the stairwell, Marcia began to head down but Reggie pulled her upward.

"There's no way out up there!" Marcia said.

"He's already below us!" Reggie said. "He'd beat us to the ground floor and be waiting for us!"

Marcia quickly saw the sense of it and the two of them ran up the one flight to the door to the roof.

The roof was flat, tar and gravel, broken up by ventilation fans, a utility hut for the building's air conditioner.

Reggie pointed Marcia to the utility hut. "Get behind there. I'll let him see me. When he does, you take off down the stairs."

"You're not gonna be a hero for me, lady!"

"Not my intention. You hit those stairs and get me help! I think I can buy time; I think I can talk to him."

"Why's he even gonna bother with you? You said *I'm* the one on his list."

"I'm on his list too."

"Jesus…"

"If you want to see your son, again, then for God's sake do what I tell you!"

Reggie was already picking up that Marcia didn't take long to process situations. Marcia nodded and ran off to hide in the shadows of the utility hut. Reggie ran to the parapet facing the Computer Sciences building. There was a police car parked out in front and it looked like the officer was standing by his car, radio microphone in his hand.

Sirens. Fire engines? No; police, but already close. Then, blue flashers just below her; Denny Petit's SUV, a magnetic blue flasher on his roof, vaulting across the quad, tires chewing deep into the sod and spitting out clods, skidding to a halt in front of the library. The policeman at the Computer Sciences building came running over.

"Denny!" she called down. "He's in here!"

He looked up, saw her, ran for the front doors, tugged at them. Locked. He stood back, covered his face with one arm for protection, drew his pistol and fired several shots through the heavy glass.

But any sense Reggie felt the crisis might have passed its peak collapsed when she heard Frank Cole's voice behind her: "It wasn't supposed to be you."

With the fire alarm, sirens, the wind cutting across the roof, she hadn't heard him step out onto the roof.

"I wasn't looking for you, Reggie. Not tonight." His face was oddly placid. In his right fist, fingers flexing around the handle, a ball peen hammer.

In the pale light of the moon, his face was death-like. She wondered, Is Frank Cole -- *my* Frank Cole -- even here right now?

"I know, Frank. But I'm here, now. You were looking for me last night, weren't you?" She crab-walked along the parapet, trying to maintain the distance between them. Maybe because she wasn't who he'd expected, he didn't close, but walked along in parallel. "I know you didn't like what I did to Denny."

"You hurt him."

"I know. I'm sorry. I told him I was sorry."

Cole nodded. "You were hurt. Someone hurt you. A long time ago. Someone who was supposed to love you but didn't. And now you're hurting Denny the same way. You're hurting my friend."

Reggie tried to look past him, across the dark roof to see if Marcia had made it to the roof door. She saw no sign of her. I've got to find *my* Frank, Reggie thought, reach *my* Frank... "You're right. I didn't understand that...but you helped me understand. *You* helped me, Frank. And you can keep helping me. Because that's what you do, isn't it? Help people heal? Like you helped people back in Philadelphia, like you've been helping the kids here."

For the first time, Cole showed some feeling on his face; a great, heavy sadness, so heavy his head sagged. "So many," he said, almost in a sob, "So many..."

"I know. But you made a difference --"

Angrily, now, his fist flexing around the handle of the hammer, holding it up in front of him. "I made a difference by...*stopping it!* In the end...in the end...that's the only way!"

Past Cole's shoulder she could see the roof door open slowly, quietly, then a broad-shouldered figure silhouetted by the moonlight, feet setting down softly on the gravel, in one hand...a pistol.

"This is not who Frank Cole is," Reggie said. "This is not the real Frank Cole, the one who helps, the one who heals, the one I saw in the video who held that girl to let her know she was safe with you. I want you to do that for me, Frank. Make me feel safe and heal me. *This...isn't...you!*"

Cole looked at the hammer as if he'd just discovered it in his hand, surprised by it, saddened by it. "I saw him do it... My father... I couldn't help my mother..."

The figure by the roof door raised his pistol, the grip cupped in both hands. Moonlight glinted silver on the badge on his breast.

"You were a child," Reggie said, "What could you do?"

Cole's chest heaved, a tremendous sigh, his voice on the edge of crying. "I stood there…afraid. I couldn't even scream." And now, cold anger: "But then I found him." And now his eyes -- those cold, angry eyes -- moved from the hammer to Reggie.

"That's over and done, Frank. Your father is dead. These kids here, they need you. *I* need you. If you do this, all you'll do is create more pain."

"It was pain that created me."

"Fight it, Frank. The way you tell these kids you help to fight it."

Reggie had been so fixed on Cole she hadn't seen the other man on the roof had been easing himself closer, he was only a few feet from Cole, his pistol still in his hand…but he hadn't fired.

Cole slapped his forehead, then slaps turned to punches. *"Why can't you let me go? For the love of God, <u>let me go</u>!"*

The policeman behind Cole lunged.

Cole heard the movement, the crunch of gravel under the press of a foot. He turned, sidestepped and Denny Petit went down on the roof, his pistol popping free from his hand, skittering across the gravel. Cole stood over Denny, his arm came up, the hammer raised high.

"Frank, no!" Reggie screamed.

Cole froze.

"He's your friend! What has *he* done?"

Cole stepped back, lowered his arm, again studied the hammer as if it was a strange alien thing. Then his face twisted in ugly hatred, and he hurled the hammer off into the night. He leaned his head back. "Dad!" he yelled into the darkness. *"I'll see you in hell!"* and he ran for the parapet.

Denny scrambled to his feet, trying to grab Cole, almost following him over the edge of the parapet, the only thing keeping him from losing his balance…Reggie grabbing him by the back of his belt.

Below, they could barely make out Frank Cole's body in the dark shadow of the library. There was a crowd down below; the fire department was there, now, an EMS rig, campus security, Denny's little police force, curious students were now coming out of their dorms and drifting across the quad. One of the other policemen knelt by Cole's broken body, looked up, shook his head.

Neither Reggie nor Denny had anything left; they both sagged, slid down the parapet, sitting on the roof with their backs against the wall. Reggie let herself fall against Denny, and after a bit felt his arm come around her shoulders.

"Marcia?" she asked, barely having the strength to speak.

"She was coming down while I was coming up. She's ok."

"How…did you know…"

"I got to Frank's house. He wasn't home. Then Monday, or Mooney, whatever the hell is name is, radioed me from Marcia's house that she wasn't home. Then I remembered when we questioned her, she said she worked at the library. I was already almost here when I heard the fire alarm."

"Denny…"

"We'll talk later. I'm going to have someone take you home. I have to stay here and take care of things."

Tiredly, he got to his feet, then reached down, took her by both hands and helped her upright.

"I feel like I can barely walk," she said.

"It can hit you like that." He put his arm around her waist. "You can lean on me," and he walked her toward the door.

Epilogue

"Voila!" Ann Bonano said and stepped back with a grand sweep of her arm toward the now refurbished chair.

Reggie smiled. "Is this still an allegory?"

"More like a half-assed Queen Ann, but if you want to make the point about reclaiming something damaged --"

"Let's not flog the imagery to death any more than we already have," Reggie laughed. "But point taken."

A car horn tooted, and Reggie turned to see Denny's SUV pulled up in front of Ann's house. She waved at Denny to wait, and turned back to Ann. "You didn't say anything about me going to this thing."

Ann picked some stray bits of lint and threads from the chair's new rich green velvet upholstery. "Because I'm not surprised."

"No?"

"I don't know you long, sweets, but I think I know you well. You figured if you didn't go, who would?" Then Ann gave her a hug and sent her on her way.

Reggie froze when she opened the door to Denny's SUV and saw him behind the wheel looking quite corporate in a three-piece gray suit. "Wow."

"I hope that's a good 'wow.'"

"It's a good 'wow'."

"It's the only one I own: my court appearance/wedding/funeral suit. I can't remember the last time I wore it. I'm surprised it still fits."

Reggie climbed in beside him. "Oh, it fits just fine."

Denny slipped the SUV into gear and they started off. "Um…"

"What?"

"Well, I don't want to be morbid…"

"What?" she said, pushing a little harder.

"I'm still trying to figure this thing out. Can you help me?"

She nodded at him to go ahead.

"It was Frank who killed his father, wasn't it?"

"Looks like it."

"But then…well, as far as we know, nothing since then. Right?"

"I think when he found his father and he -- …" Reggie found herself not wanting to put it into words. "Anyway, I'm guessing that was the catharsis he needed. When it was done…he was done."

"So, what happened? What kicked him off up here?"

"Putting on my celebrity TV shrink hat, he was working with a lot of damaged people back in Philadelphia. I think it was getting to him. I know his boss was worried about that which is why he pushed Frank to take the job up here. Same as you; a nice, quiet little town to get away from the day-in/day-out horror show back home. But also like you, he came up here and found this was no escape. All these kids he was working with... I don't want to oversimplify this, but maybe it was a matter of one damaged soul too many coming into Frank's office."

Denny shook his head. "The doctor who tried to help everybody but couldn't help himself."

Reggie sighed in agreement. "I think, at the end, he was trying to help everybody *and* himself. He stopped compartmentalizing. He wanted to stop the pain he was dishing out...and his own pain. I believe 'tragic irony' would be the right description. The very thing that made Frank -- ..." Again, the words didn't want to come. "...that made Frank...do what he did, was also why he was so good at his job. His old boss called it: empathy. He just empathized too much."

Reggie was used to the cemeteries back home; tombstones and monuments shoulder to shoulder, marching on acre after acre, generations of the countless dead. She had never seen anything like this small cemetery outside of Diamond Cove, a few dozen graves scattered around a gentle knoll surrounded by an ivy-threaded wrought iron fence. She could see, in the distance, the sun sparkling on the waters of the Atlantic.

Denny pulled to a stop in the small, graveled parking area and pointed to the knot of people gathered around an open grave in a far corner.

"Who're they?" Denny asked.

Reggie shook her head, not knowing. "I think Jonathan's here," she said, nodding at Manx's Camry parked nearby.

They walked together up the easy slope, past haphazardly strewn burial plots. Some stones were from recent years, others -- brown, thin, tilted, and cracked stones, their inscriptions barely readable -- dating back to the area's earliest settlers.

As they got closer to the grave, Reggie began to recognize some of the faces from the videos of Jonathan Manx's "inner child" sessions. "I think they're kids who dealt with Frank," she whispered.

The young people parted, opening a space for them by the open grave. The coffin -- a plain, wooden box, all that the school would pay for since Frank Cole had no living family -- sat on canvas straps. A somber-faced man in a dark suit -- the funeral director, Reggie guessed -- stood off at a discrete distance with two coveralled men with shovels. Jonathan Manx also stood off a few steps, as if acceding to the tacit request that the graveside belonged to these young people. Reggie felt the same sense and led Denny to stand with her by Manx.

A girl Reggie recognized as "Alicia" from the "inner child" sessions -- the girl she'd seen comforted by Frank Cole -- took a place at the head of the grave.

She cleared her throat, and when she spoke, her voice trembled. She looked over at Reggie, Denny, and Manx. "We didn't know if anybody from the school was gonna come. We decided one of us should say something, I said I would, unless one of you…"

Manx nodded at her to go ahead.

Alicia cleared her throat again, a finger dabbed at her eyes. "Well, ok, so, we heard some bad things about Dr. Cole. It's hard to believe but I guess they're true.

There's no way to make them not sound bad. But it's hard for us to hate him for that stuff. I suppose we should or be mad about it or somethin'. But the thing is, we're all here 'cause he helped each of us." She looked up at the circle of red-rimmed eyes, of hands holding hands. "Anyways, he tried. For some of us, he was maybe the only one who ever tried. Whatever else anybody says 'bout him, even if it's true, that's what we're gonna remember."

The funeral director stepped forward, flicked a switch on the little winch that controlled the canvas straps and Frank Cole's casket slowly lowered into the ground. Some of the young people tossed a clod of dirt down on top of the casket, others a flower, a few an envelope with some personal farewell inside; it all went into the grave with Frank Cole. As a group, they walked off.

Manx stepped to the edge of the grave, his eyes -- red eyes, Reggie noted -- fixed on the coffin below.

Reggie stood beside him. "I'm surprised to see you here," she said. "I didn't think anybody from the university would be here."

Manx grinned wryly. "There was some debate about it. In the end, they felt it would be…inappropriate."

"But you came. Worried about how your program would look?" Reggie was immediately sorry she'd said it, but before she could apologize --

"I have that coming," Manx said with a resigned nod. "The thing is Regina… Francis Cole was my friend. He was the only friend I had up here. He may have been the only real friend I've had in years." He turned to her.

"Those kids, Regina… They're going to need my help to deal with this…and I can't connect with them the way Francis did. I'm going to need help." It bordered on a plea.

She smiled and gave him a hug. "I hadn't planned on going anywhere, Jonathan."

He mumbled a thanks into her shoulder, stepped back, wiped at his eyes, gave an apologetic smile toward Denny, and headed back to his car.

Denny stepped up beside her, let his fingers intertwine with hers as they both looked down into the grave.

"Well," Denny sighed.

Reggie nodded along. "Well."

Denny asked if she'd mind stopping at the cove and she was happy to. He shucked off his jacket and vest and tie, and it almost made her laugh to see how liberated it made him feel. It was late afternoon, the sky turning a lovely late day amber. They walked hand-in-hand along the beach to the pile of rocks where she'd seen Denny that first night, smoking his forbidden cigarette. Denny took that same seat on the rocks, looking out toward the easy rolling waves. He smiled.

"Ya know, I think that sonofabitch actually cured me of my smoking." Then his face clouded. "I don't know how to feel about this. What he did was… It was horrible. But he was my friend, Reg. And he helped me." He looked to her with red-rimmed eyes, hoping for some kind of answer from her, a resolution.

"Everybody has demons, Denny. Frank lost the war with his, God help him. But I think…" And here she smiled at Denny, stepped closer to him, "I think maybe…I faced mine down." She took him by the hand, raised him up from the rocks and pulled him close.

"Reggie, I made you a promise, and I intend to keep --"

"Shut up," she said, pulled his head down and they kissed long and deeply. As she finally let her lips fall away, she could look past Denny into a sky that had suddenly gone from amber to a rich crimson. "Consider that contract nullified."

And seemingly from that same sky: "It's about goddamned time!"

They both laughed, turned, and saw Ann Bonano on her deck. Ann was holding up a cocktail class. "How'd you two like to celebrate with a drink? In honor of the young doctor from New York, I'm doing cosmos today!"

Still chuckling, they walked along the beach toward the house, hand in hand.

About the Author

Aja Holland lives on the coast of southern Maine where she teaches at a small university and loves to watch storms come in over the ocean. She shares her home with an adventurous shih-tzu and one judgmental cat. *Original Sins* is her debut novel.